THE OTHER SIDE OF LOVE

Forever Love – Book Four

J.S. COOPER

This book is a work of fiction. Names, characters, places, and incidents either are the product of the author's imagination or are used fictitiously. Any resemblance to actual persons, living or dead, events, or locales is entirely coincidental.

THE OTHER
SIDE OF LOVE

PROLOGUE

THE FIRST TIME I FULLY REALIZED that I had made a decision that was going to change my life forever was when I saw Skylar. There was something so innocent and haunting about the look in her eyes; they told me that she knew secrets of the world that I could only guess at. She watched me keenly and openly as I walked around the room, and I was worried that she wasn't going to like me. I felt tense as I waited for her to assess me. I thought I just wanted her to get to know me and to like me. I knew that it would make everything easier. I'd never counted on us having the bond that we did. I'd never counted on my heart belonging to her. I'd never felt a love like this before.

There are some people who live their lives with courage and determination. And then there are some who succumb to their emotions and crumble when they come across an obstacle. I've always tried to live my life the first way—it's the only way I know how to live. Or, rather, it was. Now I'm not so sure. Walking away without saying goodbye was the hardest thing I've ever had to do. And it was the weakest. Growing up, everyone thought that my brother, Zane, was the strong one; he was the oldest and the protector, but they didn't see the pain in his eyes that I did. They didn't know the rejection that he felt when our mother left, the rejection that created a wall around his heart thicker than the chests in Fort Knox.

Leaving him had been devastating, especially because I knew he had to think I was dead. I thought that nothing would ever be able to beat my feelings of guilt and anger the day I died. But I was wrong. Leaving her had turned out to be even more devastating. And the fact that I hadn't been able to say goodbye still tore at my heart. But I knew it was for the best.

CHAPTER ONE

"NOAH, ARE YOU HUNGRY?" LUCKY'S voice was soft as she knocked on my bedroom door, interrupting my thoughts. She sounded motherly and I laughed to myself at the irony of her looking after Zane and myself.

"A little bit." I said and then walked over to the door to open it. "Morning." I smiled down at her glowing face, and she beamed up at me. Her cheeks were rosy red and her brown eyes sparkled though her dark lashes. Her long dark hair was up in a ponytail and she looked fresh and beautiful.

"You look too beautiful for first thing in the morning." I teased her. I pulled her hair and she giggled.

"You certainly know how to make a girl happy first thing in the morning. I'll make us breakfast if you want."

"Is Zane here?" I asked casually, not wanting to answer her question until I had an answer.

"No," she shook her head and bit her lip. "He had to go out."

"I see." I tried to stifle a sigh. "So what's for breakfast, then?"

"He'll come around." She grabbed ahold of my hand and squeezed it, while her big brown eyes looked at me compassionately. "He's still hurt. But he'll get over it."

"Yeah, eventually he'll get over it and forgive me." I nodded. I knew that in my heart he would we would eventually be okay and that gave me a certain amount of hope. But *she* wouldn't. I knew that for certain. *She* would always hate me for what I had done—or what I hadn't done.

"What do you want to do today?" Lucky looked at me hopefully. "I thought we could go out and—"

"I'm sorry, but I have to go and talk to Special Agent Waldron." I lied with a straight face. It came so easily to me now; my heart rate didn't even beat faster, and the feelings of guilt were minimal.

"Oh?" She wrinkled her nose. "I thought that stuff was all taken care of now?"

"It is." I looked away. "I just need to take care of some things."

"Oh, okay." She paused. "Maybe when you get back, we can go over the documentary stuff. I'm sure Sidney must be wondering where we are."

"Maybe tomorrow?" I responded and then smiled at her. "I'm not sure how long I'll be out today."

"Oh, okay." She frowned and looked as though she wanted to ask me something else.

"So, let's go get breakfast. I'm feeling quite starved now." I ran down the stairs ahead of her, not wanting her to ask me any more questions. I liked Lucky a lot, and I didn't want to lie to her more than I had to. I watched her as she walked into the kitchen behind me. She really was a beautiful girl, and the pregnancy seemed to make her glow. With her big warm brown eyes and her long brown hair, she had already worked her way into my heart, both because she was a good person and because she loved my brother and made him happy. I had been shocked when Zane had told me he was in a relationship. In fact, I could honestly say that I was more shocked to find out that Zane had a girlfriend than he was to find out I was still alive. Okay, maybe not more shocked, but I was pretty shocked. But Lucky was great; she was perfect for my brother. There was something so warm and caring about her, and I loved her no-nonsense attitude. She obviously adored Zane, but she didn't put up with his crap either. She reminded me a bit of Skylar. I froze as her name crossed my mind. *Forget her, Noah. It's over. You have no chance of making that right.* I repeated my daily mantra to myself in my head as Lucky started to prepare breakfast.

"Omelet with peppers, onions and bacon okay?"

"Any cheese?"

"We have cheddar and Swiss."

"Let's go with cheddar." I grinned at her and jumped off of the stool I was sitting on to go over and help her. "I'll make the toast. White or wheat?"

"Let's go with sourdough." She laughed at me as I looked around the kitchen for the bread. "Look in the bread bin." She pointed at a pinewood object on the counter top.

"I had no idea there was such a thing as a bread bin." I made a goofy face and pulled out the bread and shook my head. "I guess you can tell I'm not very domesticated."

"I guess it runs in the Beaumont family." She laughed and me and handed me a knife, so I could slice the loaf.

"Well, you know. You grow up rich with maids and cooks, and you can't cook much of anything."

"I guess you can do toast and cereal." She cracked some eggs, and giggled. "Lots of yummy cereal."

"Do I look like I survive on cereal to you?" I winked at her and flexed my muscles. Lucky's eyes sparkled appreciatively as she stared at my arms and chest.

"No, you're way too built for that."

"Trying to steal my fiancée already, Noah?" Zane's slow drawl was light, but I could hear the warning in his voice. I stifled a laugh at the jealousy in his face. It was hilarious to see that my brother was so whipped.

"Zane." Lucky ran over to him, and gave him a quick peck on the lips. "You're back." She sounded happy and I watched as he kissed her nose before rubbing her belly intimately.

"I couldn't stand to be away from you," he purred back at her, and it took everything in me to not demand a DNA test right away. What had happened to my brother? "You're not feeling cold, bro?" Zane raised an eyebrow at me and gave me a once-over.

"No." I grinned at him and continued slicing the bread. I suppose it was a bit presumptuous of me to walk around in my boxers and no top, but I really hadn't thought it was a big deal.

"What are you up to today?"

"I have some stuff to do." I kept my back to him and cocked my head to look at him. "Want some toast?" I looked into his eyes, and he stared at me for a few moments without speaking. I knew he had questions for me, but I wasn't ready to answer them yet.

"Yeah, I'll have two slices." He continued to stare at me, and I knew he was telling me that he wasn't going to wait much longer to find out exactly what had gone on. I wasn't sure how to proceed, though. There was too much I didn't want him to know.

"So, when is your next doctor's appointment, Lucky?"

"Not for two weeks." She chopped the onion up carefully as she spoke. "But everything is going fine so far, so that's good."

"I can't believe I'm going to be an uncle." I shook my head and then looked at Zane. "And I sure as hell can't believe that you're going to be a dad."

"Well, you're going to have to watch your language once the babies come." He gave me a look and then laughed.

"I'm sure I can get away with saying hell for the first few years." I grinned back at him. "But, I'll keep my shits and fucks to a minimum."

"How sweet of you, bro." He rolled his eyes at me. "I can already tell you're going to be the best uncle ever."

"You know it."

"My friend Leeza is coming to visit in a few weeks." Lucky glanced at me, and I could see a blush rising on her face. "I thought maybe you guys could go to lunch one day. Because I was hoping you guys would both be godparents."

"Oh, no way is Leeza going to be a godparent to my child." Zane's voice was loud. "And I'm not having her as a sister-in-law, either."

"Zane." Lucky's face was a deep red now. "Don't be mean."

"I'm just being honest." He shrugged.

"I think Noah might like her." Lucky pouted at him.

"I think not." Zane gave her a look. "I'm not having that crazy ho around my brother."

"Zane!" Lucky poked him in the chest.

"I'm still here, guys." I raised a hand. "No need to talk about me like I'm not."

"Well, you never know," Zane drawled, and I ignored him. "One day you're here and the next you're gone."

"I'd be happy to meet your friend, Lucky, but I'm not on the dating market right now. My heart isn't really open to loving anyone else at this moment in time." A dart of pain ripped through my heart and I held on to the counter tightly.

"You okay?" Lucky looked at me in concern.

"Yeah, I'm fine. Thanks." I turned away from her and nodded. I had to be fine. There was nothing else I could do. Skylar was gone from my life forever. I'd made that decision two months ago when I had walked away. And now—now I was out of that life, and there was no going back. Even though that life had felt more real than anything I'd ever felt before. She had wormed her way in and had never left.

"He most probably had a premonition of what life would be like if he dated Leeza." Zane patted me on the shoulder and gave me his 'we need to talk soon' look.

"Zane, you're horrible. She's not that bad."

"She's not that bad?" His voice was incredulous. "She's a snake, and I'm sure she would have bedded me if she could have."

"She wouldn't do that to me."

"Lucky, she would have done me in a heartbeat. She was all over me. I mean, come on, how could she resist?"

"Idiot." She slapped him on the shoulder and laughed. "I know she hasn't been the best friend, but I want to give her another chance."

"Eh."

"I mean if it wasn't for her getting me to the party, we might not be together now."

"I would have thought of something." Zane stood behind her and wrapped his arms around her waist. "There was no way I was going to let you out of my life." He bent his head and nuzzled on her neck, and I watched as Lucky squirmed in his arms.

"Not now." She squealed as he squeezed her behind and I took that as a signal to leave the room.

"Hey, guys, call me when it's ready." I laughed and Lucky blushed as I walked out of the kitchen and back up the stairs. I smiled as I walked up the stairs. Lucky wasn't the sort of girl that I thought Zane would end up with, and I was glad. I had long worried that he'd end up with some ice queen who looked stunning but had poison running through her veins. Thank God, he and I had both escaped from Angelique's clutches. I ran into my room as I heard my phone ringing and grabbed it quickly.

"Hello."

"Noah?"

"Sidney?"

"Yes. It's me." He paused, and I could hear Betty whispering in the background. "Zane told me you were back, but I wasn't sure. Sorry about the background noise. Betty wanted to know if you were okay."

"No worries." I smiled into the phone while listening to my old friend's voice. "Tell her I'm well."

"I hope you'll be telling her in person soon." Sidney chuckled. "She can't barely believe you came back from the dead."

"You didn't tell Betty?" I was shocked.

"You told me not to tell anyone."

"But I assumed you would tell Betty."

"I wanted to, but Betty likes to talk. You know women, I didn't want to ruin anything."

"Oh, Sidney," I sat on my bed, and closed my eyes. "Thank you."

"I'm glad you're safe. I've missed you."

"I've missed you, too." I felt emotional. Sidney Johnson had become like a father to me. He was the only person who knew most of my secrets. There was no one who knew all of them but he was the closest.

"I've still got your papers." He spoke in a low voice. "Are you going to tell Zane?"

"He doesn't need to know." I lowered my voice as well.

"He went to France."

"I heard."

"She turned him away."

"She shouldn't have done that." I was angry. "I'll have to call her."

"You sure you want to do that?"

"No, not really." I lay back and rubbed my temples. I was starting to get a headache. "But I need to know what she said to him."

"You should tell him."

"No." I shook my head vehemently. "He's in a good place now. I don't want to disturb that."

"Noah, I know you think you're protecting him, but he has a right to know. And honestly, I don't think he's going to just let it go. He has a right to know the truth about his past."

"I'll tell him something." I cleared my throat. "Anyways, how have you been? I heard Lucky has been working on the documentary with you."

"I've been good. Better since Lucky and Zane been coming over; made me not worry about you so much. Lucky's a good girl." Sidney sighed. "I like her a lot, she's good for your brother. She really loves him."

"I know. I'm glad he met her."

"What about you? You got anyone?"

"No." *Not anymore.*

"What about where you were hidden out?"

"I dated. Nothing too serious." *Liar.*

"You're still young. Plenty of fish in the sea."

"Yeah. I'm not too worried."

"What about the girl you mentioned to me? When you first got there?" Sidney talked slowly. "The one I told you to be careful with."

"You were right to warn me to be careful." I sighed deeply. "Things got complicated. Her life was complicated."

"Were you one of the complications?"

"I became one of them." I stared at the wall as I spoke. "My presence ended up hurting someone."

"Nothing bad, I hope."

"I hope not." I lowered my voice. "I was going to ask you later, but I need you to speak to your son for me. The family attorney. I have some questions."

"You in trouble?"

"No." I shook my head as I bit my lip. "Not yet."

"You're scaring me. Why do you sound like you're about to leave us again, Noah? You should be happy, you just got back."

"I'm back, but everything isn't the same as it was before, Sidney. My life didn't stop when I went away. Life continued for you and for me. New complications arose. I guess there are troubles to be left and to be found."

"Where did you go?"

"I can't say."

"You mean you won't say."

"Yeah." There was no need to lie to Sidney; he knew the deal. "I'll talk about it later. I don't want to think about it now."

"Lucky got some good ideas for the documentary. She's a history buff like you. She knows a lot about civil rights." Sidney changed the subject and I smiled to myself. He always knew how to read me.

"I'm excited to hear them."

"Yes. It will be good to get your life back on track." Sidney paused again. "I'm glad you're back, you know."

"I know." I couldn't stop myself from smiling into the phone, even though I knew he couldn't see me. "I'm glad to be back as well." I hung up and looked up slowly to see Lucky staring at me from the doorway with a half-smile.

"Hey, I just wanted to let you know that breakfast was ready."

"Thanks." I nodded and remained seated and she walked into the room uncertainly.

"Do you have someone that you left behind?" She chewed on her bottom lip and stared into my eyes earnestly. "Asides from Zane, I mean. Did you leave a girlfriend behind? We just assumed that Angelique was the girl you were seeing, because you know, you were devastated by her dumping you." She made a face. "Thank God that wasn't true. But was there someone else?" She took a deep breath, as she stopped rambling and she looked into my eyes searchingly but slightly hesitantly. I could tell that she felt like she was prying a little bit and wasn't sure if she was stepping over the line.

"I wasn't seeing anyone seriously when I left." I shrugged. "But you're right, Angelique wasn't the love of my life by any means."

"I wonder why she believed that you were so in love with her that you would take your life." Lucky frowned. "I mean, if she hadn't believed that one point, everything could have been ruined."

"Angelique would believe she was an angel from heaven if you told her that." I laughed. "She wasn't low in self-confidence."

"I guess that's true." Lucky sat down next to me. "Are you okay, Noah? I know that Zane has been a little distant, and we haven't really asked you how you're doing. We've been so happy to see you alive that we haven't really thought about anything else. But I assume you've had a life the last year or so, away from here. It must have been hard to start over and then have to leave."

"It wasn't hard." I jumped up as my stomach growled. "Zane has always been the first person in my thoughts, and it was never my intention for him to think I was dead and gone this long. I couldn't stay there when I knew that Zane was out here with a hole in his heart."

"You're the first person in his life, too." Lucky walked with me to the door. "I don't know that I've ever seen the light in his eye that returned when you came back from the dead."

"Not anymore." I spoke matter-of-factly, and I saw Lucky's face drop. I grabbed ahold of her hands and stopped her at the top of the stairs. "My brother loves you, and I'm not sad that you are his main concern now. That's how it should be. That's how true love should be. I'm still his brother and he will always love me, but you're the one he lives for." The words were passionate on my lips, and I laughed as I realized that Zane had figured it all out before me. Oh, the irony of the situation was fantastic. It hurt just like a knife had been stabbed into my heart and twisted, and I stood still for a moment as I absorbed the unspoken grief and loss that sat in me.

"Noah." Lucky's eyes flashed with concern and she grabbed my shoulders as I refocused on her. "We're going to have to talk. Maybe not today and maybe not tomorrow. But someday, you're going to talk to me. Because the worst thing you can do is keep your worries to yourself."

"Okay." I nodded and then smiled. "Thank you."

"No worries." She grinned at me as my stomach growled. "Now, let's go get you some food."

CHAPTER TWO

"THIS IS WHERE PEOPLE GO WHEN they want to disappear." She didn't smile as she looked me over slowly and intently. "No one else moves to Palm Bonita."

"I didn't move here because I wanted to disappear." I shrugged and stared into her eyes confidently. I stood in the alleyway and wondered who this woman was who had just walked up to me out of the blue.

"Maybe you didn't want to disappear, but you had to." Her eyes issued me a challenge and I hid my surprise. She was

smarter than I thought she would be. But to be honest, my thoughts weren't based on anything other than her looks. She looked too beautiful to be intelligent. I suppose a feminist would kill me for saying that, but then again, I wouldn't say it out loud. I knew that my thoughts were based on my own masculinity, but based on her looks I thought she'd be an airhead. She had long white-blonde hair and big doleful blue eyes that glittered at me with an emotion akin to distaste.

"Perhaps."

"I know guys like you." She laughed and shook her head. "You think you know me just by my looks, but let me tell you, mister, you know absolutely nothing about me."

"I think you've got it a bit twisted. You were the one claiming to know me, not the other way around."

"No, I was just the honest one. I spoke my thoughts out loud." She turned around then and walked away from me. I hurried up to catch her, feeling confused and annoyed at myself for getting off on the wrong foot already with someone in my new town.

"Hey, wait, I'm sorry." I grabbed ahold of her shoulder and she flinched, glaring at me as she pulled away quickly.

"Don't touch me."

"I didn't mean to scare you." My eyes narrowed, and this time I looked at her for a longer period of time. I studied her face carefully this time; I tried to look beyond the surface of her perfect features. Her eyes looked red and puffy as if she had been crying a lot, and her lips looked cracked under her lip gloss. Her cheekbones seemed too pronounced for her face, and her clothes hung on her body as if they were too big. She was either wearing someone else's clothes or she had lost a lot of weight recently.

"You didn't scare me."

"So why did you want to disappear?" I smiled at her weakly, and her eyes flashed at me, looking me over in distrust.

"So you admit it, you came here to get away?"

"I'm dead." I laughed, but no smile crossed my face.

"I'm dead too." She nodded and ran her hands through her hair. She had understood exactly what I meant.

"I'm Noah." I reached out my hand to shake hers. "I mean, I'm Mikey."

"It's best not to use any names." Her handshake was firm, but her fingers felt soft and cold. I wanted to rub them between mine, to warm her up. "It's safer that way."

"How long have you been here?"

"Three months." Her voice lowered. "And if I were you, I wouldn't ask too many people too many questions. Most of us didn't come here to get away from something bad."

"What do you mean?" I frowned, not really sure what she meant.

"Most of the people in Palm Bonita are the bad. They have come here to disappear so that they won't be caught."

"Oh." I pursed my lips. "Well, that means we good guys should stick together."

"Who said I was one of the good ones?" She raised an eyebrow, and walked away from me and back down the alley. I watched her as she walked away again. She stopped after a few yards and looked back at me.

"Be careful, Noah." She placed a finger against her lips. "Be very careful."

I sat on the couch, holding my phone, thinking about the first time I met *her* when Zane walked into the living room. He stood there staring at me for a few moments, and I laughed.

"Don't tell me the cat has your tongue." I shook my head. "This is the first time I've actually seen you stand and think before spouting off whatever you wanted to tell me."

"Blame Lucky." He laughed as well, and sat down on the couch next to me.

"More like thank her."

"There's that as well." His eyes crinkled as he thought of his fiancée, and I envied him the peace of mind and stability she had brought to his life. I wanted that for myself, but I also wanted to make sure that nothing interrupted the new joy that Zane had in his life.

"What were you thinking about just now?" Zane's tone became thoughtful. "You looked so far away just now."

"I was just thinking about the day I moved to Palm Bonita."

"Palm Bonita? Is that were you where?" Zane stared at me. "Is that here in California?"

I shook my head. "No, it's a small town in Florida, about an hour south of Orlando."

"I see. Did you choose the area?"

I shook my head and almost chuckled to myself. "Agent Waldron suggested it might be a good place for me to go and lie low as I didn't want to become a part of the witness protection program."

"Wait, what?" Zane's eyebrows furrowed. "What are you talking about? I thought you were in witness protection?"

"I wasn't an official part of the program." I shrugged and looked away from him. "Once you go in, you can't really come out. I wasn't willing to close the door."

"So you did it for me?" Zane's lips thinned. "You risked your safety for me, yet you couldn't or wouldn't tell me what your plan was."

"I don't want to go through this again." I let out a big sigh. "Not now, please."

"So what happened the day you moved to Palm Bonita?"

"Honestly?" I laughed. "I wondered what the fuck I had done and wanted to call the whole thing off."

"It was that good, then?" Zane gave me a half-smile, but his eyes looked me over with concern. No matter how angry he was at me, I was still his brother, and he was still concerned about my feelings more than anything.

"Better." I rolled my eyes. "Palm Bonita is one of those nowhere, small dusty towns, where ex-gang bosses and mafiosi go to spend their days."

"Sounds delightful."

"Yeah. It was an adjustment." My thoughts drifted back to the decrepit apartment building I had found myself living in. It was cockroach- and rat-infested, but even worse than that was the smell. The stench of rotting eggs and hidden fish had filled the complex, and no amount of spray or candles had diminished it.

"Want to tell me more over lunch?" Zane looked at me hopefully, and I nodded. There were many things I couldn't tell him, but I knew that he would want to know about my time away. And as long as I kept to the bare minimum, everything should be okay.

"The sky looks beautiful today." Lucky walked into the living room with some recently picked flowers and my face turned white. "You okay?"

"Yeah," I jumped up. "I thought you said something else. That's all." I gave her a weak smiled and I noticed Lucky and Zane exchanging a worried glance. "I'm okay, guys."

"No one said you weren't." Zane grabbed Lucky's hand, and pulled her towards him. "Noah and I are going to lunch, want to come?"

"If Noah doesn't mind." She looked at me eagerly, and I tried not to laugh. She was so different than the type of girl I had imagined seeing Zane with.

"I don't mind. I'm pretty sure whatever I tell my brother, he shares with you anyway."

"Zane can keep a secret." Lucky blushed, while my brother glared at me.

"I'm just joking, guys. It's fine. I don't expect you to hide anything from each other. Secrets ruin relationships."

"Yeah, they do." Zane gave me a pointed look and I jumped up and turned towards the stairs. I had walked into that trap, and I didn't want to stay around and feel guilted into revealing information I wasn't ready to share.

"You guys choose a place for lunch, I'm just going to go upstairs and get my stuff ready."

"What stuff?" Zane's voice was curious, and I smiled at Lucky as she pulled him away from me, whispering something about wanting his help choosing out a crib for the babies.

***

"Hi, I'm Robin and I'm going to be your waitress today. Can I start you off with any drinks?" The girl in front of me was gorgeous and I couldn't help but to admire her body. I gave her a once-over and I realized that she had caught me as I looked back up and she was glaring at me. As our eyes connected, I felt a spark of recognition light up my heart. I'd never seen this girl before, but something about her had ignited a feeling of warmth inside of me. "I'm not on the menu by the way." The smile fell from her face as she spoke to me and I wondered what had gotten her so upset. She looked away and the buzz in my ears faded.

"I didn't think that you were." I frowned at her in confusion.

"Well, the way you were looking at me made me think that perhaps you thought something else was on the menu."

"Um, okay?" I looked at Zane to see if I had missed something. Had I said something and not realized it, or was this chick just crazy?

"No, it's not okay. How would you like it if I looked at you like you were a juicy steak and I was a dog ready to pounce?" Her frown lifted and her expression changed to one of excitement and anticipation, she looked me over slowly and licked her lips before locking eyes with mine. "Not a very nice feeling, is it? To be treated like a piece of meat."

"Actually, I don't mind." I laughed and leaned towards her. "It makes me feel quite excited, actually."

"Noah." Lucky's voice sounded shocked and she shook her head at me.

"I'm just being honest." I shrugged.

"Typical male reaction." Robin shook her head and turned towards Lucky. "Anything I can get you guys?"

"We'll have three waters, please, Robin." Lucky smiled at her widely and we were all silent as Robin walked away.

"Okay, is it me or is that chick crazy?" I exclaimed as soon as Robin was out of earshot.

"Noah." Lucky laughed and made a small face. "I mean, she does seem like she is having a bad day."

"She's off." Zane shook his head. "Like loony-bin off."

"Right? What was up with that?" I rolled my eyes. "I thought she was going to grab a knife and stab me and for what?"

"Well, you did give her a once-over." Lucky smiled at me. "Some girls don't like that."

"I looked at her and appreciated her beauty," I coughed into my hand as Robin returned to the table with three waters. "I thought waitresses were meant to treat their customers like royalty, not like shit."

"Are you talking about me?" Robin raised one eyebrow at me, and our eyes met again. She had the most unusual hazel eyes; they seemed to change from brown to green to match her temperament.

"Do you see another waitress in the vicinity?"

"I prefer to be called a server."

"And?"

"Noah." Lucky's voice sounded shocked, and I saw her poke Zane in the stomach to get him to say something to me. I looked at Zane and his eyes were sparkling back at me. I could tell that he thought the whole situation was hilarious.

"It's okay. I'm used to dealing with spoiled rich boys who don't respect the help."

"Whoa, what?" I frowned up at her and swallowed hard as I stared at her beautiful shimmering eyes. She was beautiful, and I had a hard time not feeling captivated by her. Her long black hair hung straight down her back, and her sun-kissed olive skin glowed in the bright light of the restaurant.

"Nothing." She sighed and bit her lip. "I apologize for my words. It's been a long day." She looked away from me and back at Lucky. "Do you guys know what you want to order yet?"

"We're going to share the bleu cheese burger with a large fries, please." Zane spoke quickly, and Lucky gave him a look.

"Who said we were sharing anything?"

"I thought you wanted—"

"You didn't even ask me if I wanted the bleu cheese burger." Lucky made a face at Robin. "Sorry, but can you give us a few minutes?"

"Sure." Robin smiled back at her briefly and gave me a look before walking away from the table.

"I think she likes you, bro." Zane winked at me and I shook my head.

"Yeah, right."

"I bet she wants to take you in the back and—"

"Zane!" Lucky's voice was impatient. "Is that what you thought about me when you first starting coming to Lou's?"

"Of course." He grinned. "I knew you wanted to do me the first day you met me."

"You're gross." Lucky punched him in the arm. "More like you wanted to do me."

"Of course." He laughed. "I saw you doing the cha cha cha, and I was hooked."

"I was learning salsa steps." Lucky smiled at him indulgently.

"Yeah, whatever." Zane pulled her towards him and kissed her. "I don't care what steps you were doing, all I knew was that I wanted to be the one you were doing them with."

"So you wanted me to take you to the back and have my wicked way with you."

"I would have been overjoyed." He grinned.

"What about your date?"

"What about her?" He laughed again and kissed her on the nose. "Now, what's this about you not wanting to share a bleu cheese burger? I thought you loved them."

"I do love them and we can share, but you can't just place an order and expect that I'm going to be okay with it without you asking me first."

"Are you joking right now?" Zane's eyes popped open and he spoke slowly. "You do want to share and you do want the bleu cheese burger, but you sent Robin away because you wanted to be difficult."

"I wasn't being difficult," Lucky rolled her eyes at him. "I wanted you to ask …"

"Okay, okay." Zane raised his hand and put on a puppy-dog face as he cut her off. "I get it."

"You guys done?" I interrupted them both. "I've a feeling Robin is going to have a heart attack if we don't order and get out of here soon."

"She does seem a little bit intense." Lucky giggled and made a face.

"Hey, guys, are you ready?" Robin walked back up to the table and dropped off a basket of bread. "I thought you guys could have some French rolls on the house."

"I told you. She wants you." Zane mouthed at me and I tried not to laugh. "You should ask her out."

"Ask her out to do what? Kill me?"

"Ask her out on a d-a-t-e."

"Yeah, right." I grimaced. "That's never going to happen."

"I have a friend that you may ..." Lucky started and Zane gave her a look. "Okay, okay. Leeza's out." She half sighed and gave me a smile. "So what kind of girls do you like, Noah?"

"Ones that don't want to kill me." I joked, but I couldn't laugh. My mind drifted back to Palm Bonita and Skylar. I could still see the pain in her eyes at our last meeting. I'd never forget our last conversation.

"Do you love me?" Her words were soft but sharp, as her eyes had stared into mine with intensity.

"I love you." I had said simply and honestly.

"Then take me with you." She'd pleaded, and her eyes were moist.

"I can't do that." I shook my head and turned away from her.

"I hate you," she'd whispered, and then she'd pushed past me and run away from me. I hadn't tried to stop her, even though I had wanted to. I wanted to run after her and beg her to understand that my decision wasn't one I wanted to make. It was one I had to make. But I knew that in her world, it didn't make a difference. I'd broken her heart and betrayed her, like every other man. And I'd just walked away. That was the thing with love: sometimes, no matter how badly you wanted to be with someone and take care of them, there were obstacles that were beyond your control. Sometimes you had to know when to walk away.

"Noah, you okay?" Lucky reached across the table and squeezed my hand. I looked up at her and blinked a few times to remember my bearings. "You drifted away there for a moment."

"Sorry." I said weakly, all humor gone from my tone. "I was just remembering someone."

"Someone special?" Lucky and Zane both looked at me with curious expressions, and I was about to answer when Robin came back to the table. I waited until she had taken our orders before I continued.

"A girl I met while I was away." I nodded. "The day I arrived, actually."

"Will you tell us about her and about Palm Bonita?" Lucky bit her lower lip and stared at me searchingly, hoping that I was willing to give some answers.

"Palm Bonita is one of those cities that you think of when you think of old Wild West movies." I stared at her, as I started talking. "It's this small town that seems to be stuck in the early 1940s. There's this air of terror and anarchy in the city. Nobody cares about rules, yet nobody wants to be seen to not care about the rules. The people who move to Palm Bonita are the dregs of the country."

"You moved there and you're not the ..." Lucky started and I smiled at her ruefully.

"I'm not a saint, but you're right, I didn't fit in with the other people who had made Palm Bonita their home. And they could tell." I sighed as I thought back to my many acrimonious interactions with people from Palm Bonita. "But I met someone pretty early on, and she was a bright light in a very dark town. A town that was made darker because I was in a bad spot in my life." I stared at Zane. "I'm still not sure if I made the right decision by doing what I did, but it's all done now. I can't change it."

"If that's an apology, it's pretty weak, Noah." Zane raised his eyebrows at me and I knew he still hadn't forgiven me.

"It's not an apology. I'm just saying I was in a bad place when I got to Palm Bonita. I wasn't sure how long I would have to stay there, and it was a weird experience having to disappear." My eyes glazed over as I spoke and thought about the loneliness and boredom that occupied my mind in the first few months. "Anyways, I met someone and she gave me some hope, and a life. We became friends and pretty quickly we became more than that. But she wasn't who I thought she was."

"A wolf in sheep's clothing, huh?"

"No," I shook my head. "She was a wolf in wolf's clothing." I laughed bitterly. "She didn't try and hide who she was. I was the idiot for thinking she was someone different."

"But you fell in love?" Lucky interrupted me with a curious tone. "You fell in love in Palm Bonita, right?"

"You could say that. I prefer to say that my heart was captured." I cleared my throat and gave her a sorrowful smile. "Because what's love, really? What does it mean? What does it matter if you can't help the ones you love?"

"You can't change anyone. Not if they don't want to be changed." Lucky reached out and grabbed ahold of my hand again and squeezed it. "You know that right, Noah?"

"I do." I caressed her hand in mine and gave her a grateful smile. "You're wonderful, you know that, right?"

"Hold on there, brother." Zane gave me a look. "We may be family, but no flirting with my girl."

"My name's Lucky." She rolled her eyes, but I saw her reach her other hand down and squeeze his thigh. "Not 'my girl.'"

"Treat her right or you may have some competition." I winked at Lucky as I spoke and her eyes sparkled back at me.

"You want to be a dad to my children?" Zane grinned at me. "I don't mind if you want to take on diaper duty."

"I think that when you love someone and you have a good heart, it shouldn't matter who the biological parents are." My tone became very serious. "So yes, if it came to it, I could love both of your children as my own very easily and I would take care of them as my own."

"Whoa, hold on there." Zane's eyes narrowed. "It seems like you've already given this some thought."

"No, not really. I just think that people in general should be more loving. And that I could easily be a father to another man's kids; maybe even a better father than the biological father." I smiled at him weakly and then continued. "Why can't we all be open and loving to everyone?"

"Good point." Zane cleared his throat. "I was hoping you'd say something like that because I would really like to know what you know about Mom and why she ignored me in Paris."

"I …"

"I don't want any bullshit answers from you, Noah." His voice rose and his tone changed. "I've had about enough waiting to find out some answers."

"Zane!" Lucky admonished him and shook her head in worry.

"No, stop sticking up for him. You're my fiancée. You should be supporting me. I want to know what's going on. I want to know why Mom left and how long Noah has known the truth. I'm done with secrets in this family." He turned away from Lucky and stared at me. "You owe me some answers, Noah. Not some bullshit philosophical thoughts about life and families. I don't give two shits about how things would be in your ideal world. I want to know the truth about our very real, un-ideal world, and I want to know now."

We stared at each other for a few moments and I wasn't sure what to say. I didn't want to tell him the truth. I knew the truth would hurt far more than me keeping it a secret. Even if it made me the bad guy. Even if it meant he had to hate me for a little bit longer. I didn't want to risk him going through all those years of pain and rejection again. I could still picture the pain in his eyes when anyone asked him where his mom was. I could still see him as a young boy crying in his bed when he thought no one was around. I could still see the hope in his eyes when the doorbell rang and we still thought our mom was going to come back. And I could still remember the angry, bitter man who couldn't get over the fact that we had been abandoned. The man that had sworn he would never fall in love, never get caught in that trap. And as I looked at him across the table with Lucky, his beautiful wonderful fiancée, who was starting to show her pregnancy in her stomach and face, and I watched the open and easy love he had for her, I knew I couldn't risk it. I couldn't risk him clamming up and reverting back to his old self.

"So tell me, Noah. What's the big secret you've been trying to keep to yourself?"

"Hey, excuse me, guys." Robin approached the table with a slightly embarrassed expression. "Can you keep it down a bit?" She stared at me with an expression of curiosity.

"Sorry." I nodded as I looked back at her with a blank expression as she attempted a small smile at me. I wasn't in the mood for her hot-and-cold games. I was fed up with girls and their games. No matter how beautiful they were.

"I'm sorry about earlier. I think I was a bit ..."
She blushed as she mumbled on to me and I waved my
hand at her.

"Forget about it. It really doesn't matter. Just give
us the check, please."

"Is there anything else you guys would like? You
haven't even gotten your—"

"Just the check, please." We stared at each other
for another moment and she nodded. "Sure, I'll be right
back." She hurried away and I watched her walk up to
the counter to print out our receipt. She had an air about
her that was slightly mysterious and intriguing. I couldn't
put my finger on it, but she was unique and had
somehow wormed her way into my already-
overcrowded mind.

"Don't think this is over," Zane leaned towards
me and whispered in a low voice. "You may have been
saved by the waitress this time, but next time you won't
be so lucky."

"Give it a break, Zane." I sighed. "Please, just give
it a break. Okay." I pulled out some twenties and placed
them on the table before jumping out of the booth. "I'm

going to walk home, I'll see you guys later." I hurried away from the table and I saw Robin turn around and watch me as I left the table. I turned around to thank her as I exited, but a weird feeling filled me as we made eye contact, and I felt flustered and uncomfortable. I nodded and mumbled a quick "thanks" before hightailing it out of the restaurant and walking down the street. I needed to think and plan. I knew that Zane was not going to let this rest. And I also knew that I couldn't allow him to know the truth. But I didn't want to lose him as well. Not after Skylar; the pain that remained in my heart from leaving her was still almost too much to bear.

***

"Hey," I knocked on the study door and walked in without waiting for Zane to grant me access. "What you up to?"

"Balancing the checkbook." Zane shrugged as he looked up at me from his table.

"Sounds fun."

"Yeah, it's a bundle of delight. Almost as much fun as disappearing to a small town in Florida."

"Yeah, that was great fun."

"I'm surprised you came back, what with your great love still being there and all."

"Sarcasm doesn't suit you."

"I'm sorry that you think that." He turned back to his computer. "I'm kind of busy."

"Is that a hint to leave?"

"I won't stop you if you walk out the door." He started tapping on the keys in front of him and I walked over to the table.

"Hey." I sat down in the dark mahogany chair.

"Yes?" He looked up at me in irritation.

"Really?" I rolled my eyes at him. "We're going to play this game?"

"I don't know what you're talking about."

"I know you're mad at me. I understand that. I didn't expect you to just forgive me when I got back. But this—this weird, rude sarcasm, this is not what I expected. Shout at me if you must, scream, whatever. Just don't treat me like some random person you don't know and don't like."

"But I don't really know you, do I?" He frowned at me. "And it's not like you trust me or care about my feelings. You didn't tell me you were working for the FBI, you won't tell me about our mom. I mean, come on, Noah, what sort of brothers are we?"

My breath caught at his words and I stared into his blazing eyes with my heart pounding.

"Do you think it was easy for me to just walk away without telling you? Do you think it didn't keep me up at night? Do you think I didn't want to call you every single morning and every single night? It fucking killed me, Zane. I wanted to tell you so badly."

"So why didn't you? You told others. Do you know how much that hurt me?"

"I don't know why she told you I told her." I said angrily. "I—"

"Who is *she*?" Zane frowned at me. "I was talking about Sidney."

"Oh." *Fuck.* "That's what I meant …"

"No, it isn't. Who is she? Who else did you tell?" Zane starred at me with a shocked and incredulous expression. "I know you're not talking about Mrs.

Johnson, but who else is there? Wait." Zane's expression changed to anger as realization dawned. "Are you talking about Mom? Did you tell Mom?"

My face turned red and he looked at me in confusion. "So you've been in contact with her? To the point where you would tell her about leaving?"

"It's not like that." I shook my head and my tone was bleak.

"What is it like, Noah?"

"Have you ever loved someone so much that you've walked away because that is the only thing you can do to protect them?"

"What?" He looked at me in confusion. "What are you talking about?"

"When I left, all I could think about was you. I knew that you would be devastated. We were all we had. And you've looked after me my whole life. You've been the best big brother ever. And you've always tried to protect me. Even when I didn't need protecting. Well, I had to protect you as well."

"You weren't protecting me by leaving and making me think you were dead, and you sure aren't protecting me by not telling me about Mom. I'm not a baby, Noah. I don't need you to hold my hand while you rip off the Band-Aid. Fucking pull that shit off and let it burn."

"Going to Palm Bonita without telling you was one of the hardest things I've ever had to do in my life. I wasn't skipping and singing songs, delighting in the fact that I pulled the wool over your eyes. But I couldn't just do nothing. They killed people, Zane. I was young and dumb and maybe I handled it incorrectly, but when Agent Waldron told me this was the only solution, I believed him. I had to give up everything. When I moved, I had nothing and no one and no one to talk to."

"I'm sorry." Zane's eyes looked bleak. "I can't profess to know what it was like."

"It was hard. There were some days where I didn't even make it out of bed because I didn't care. I was in this limbo. I had nowhere to go, nothing to do, no one to talk to."

"How did you get out of that funk?"

"One day, I met someone. She knew right away that I wasn't like most of the other people in town."

"Is this the girl you fell in love with?" Zane questioned me, and a dart of pain shot through my heart.

"She's the girl that broke my heart into pieces." I shook my head. "We're powerless, you know, when it comes to love. No matter what type of love it is. You can love someone wholly and completely as a wife, a mother, a sister, a daughter, a friend. But none of it matters. At the end of the day, it doesn't matter if you want to do the right thing and take care of someone. Sometimes there are external factors that will do everything in their power to stop you from making something right."

"So this woman that you met? She's the one that gave you hope? Did someone stop you from being with her?"

"I thought she was a victim when I first met her. I thought she was hiding out from an abusive ex. The first time I met her, she told me to be careful in the town. She told me there were a lot of bad people. I should have taken her at her word. She warned me from the beginning."

"Did someone hurt you?" Zane clenched his fist.

"Not physically." I shook my head and closed my eyes as memories came pouring in from my early days in Palm Bonita. The second time I'd seen her she was in the grocery store, studying the labels on milk. "I'd recommend the whole milk." I smiled at her as I walked over to her. "People like to recommend the two percent or one percent because it has less fat, but whole milk is a lot better for your bones." She'd stared at me for a minute without talking before grabbing a bottle of one percent. "I see you take advice well." I continued with a quick smile and grabbed a bottle of whole milk.

"I didn't ask you for any advice." Her eyes smirked at me. "I make my own decisions." She walked away from me and down to the produce aisle. For some reason I followed her and picked up some bananas as she grabbed some apples. She looked over at me and shook her head before walking up to me. "I thought I told you to be careful in this town?" Her voice was low and she looked around the store to see if there was anyone watching us as she spoke.

"I don't take advice well, either." I grinned at her, and she laughed. This time the laugh hit her eyes and her whole face was transformed with beauty as she smiled at me in genuine humor.

"Would you like to come over for dinner tonight?" she'd asked me lightly as if it were no big deal, and I had accepted eagerly and happily, not knowing that that invitation was going to change my whole life. A carton of milk had changed my life.

"Noah, you okay?" Zane's voice interrupted my thoughts and I nodded.

"Yeah, yeah. Sorry." I sighed. "I was just remembering the day she let me into her life."

"You still miss her?" His eyes searched mine.

"No, I don't miss her." I shook my head honestly.

"But you still think about her a lot." He wasn't asking a question, but I still nodded.

"Everything changed in my life when I met her and she brought me into her life. I was no longer the boy morphing into the man. I became the man." I spoke with conviction. "She made me a man."

"That's a good thing, isn't it?" Zane looked at me thoughtfully. "Lucky made me realize that I was still acting like a boy a lot of the time. She brought out the man in me; all I want to do is love her and protect her. That's what we're made for, you know. To look after our women and to love them as best as we can."

"I'm glad that Lucky has brought the love back into your life." I answered him honestly. "Family is so important.   I'm glad you've added someone else to our small group."

"We missed out on a lot, didn't we?" Zane sighed. "No mother, no father to talk of. No real love. We had nothing. I'm surprised we turned out this well."

"We'll always have each other." I grabbed his arm and squeezed it tightly.

"That's all we can really ask for, isn't it?" He nodded slowly. "To have a family that truly loves and accepts us."

"That's all that matters." I agreed. "You made a good pick with Lucky, she's amazing and I already love her like she's a part of the family."

"Yeah, I've been blessed." His eyes shone with emotion. "I'm glad you love her; she's already the central part of our family. She loves you like a brother, you know. She really loves and cares about you. It's funny that you're not even related, but she always talks and worries about you."

"I guess you don't have to be related by blood to love someone as a family member." I stared at him, my eyes blazing. "Sometimes they worm their way into your heart and they become a part of you. And when someone becomes a part of you, they automatically become your family."

CHAPTER THREE

"YOU CAN'T TELL ANYONE."

"I just need to tell my brother." I made a face. "He's a hothead, but he's trustworthy. He won't tell anyone. Not even our dad."

"No." Special Agent Waldron shook his head. "If we go forward with this, you can't tell anyone."

"I can't just leave and not tell him." My heart stilled. "It would kill him. I'm all he has."

"That's what we're counting on." He stared at me with blank eyes. "You cannot tell him."

"You don't understand. It's always been us. We don't have a mother, our father doesn't care about us. And Zane, well, he's already closed off. I can't just leave and not have him know. He won't stop searching for me."

"Then you'll die." He nodded and took out a pad. "That's probably the better idea anyway."

"Die?" I shrunk back and shivered. "I don't think Braydon knows that I heard anything. Do you think they're going to put a hit out on me?"

"I don't mean that Sanchez is going to kill you." He looked up at me and sighed. "I mean we'll fake your death. It should motivate your brother to help us."

"What do you mean?"

"I mean, he's in that crowd as well. He knows Braydon, Angelique, and the others. I'll approach him at the funeral and see if he can help me."

"I don't want him involved." I shook my head. "If you need help, I can do it."

"No." He shook his head vehemently. "They'll suspect you too easily. We need someone else."

"I don't want Zane involved in this." I stood up. "Sorry, but I'm not interested in helping anymore."

"Stop." His voice was commanding, and I paused as I walked to the door. "It's not safe for you or anyone else. We need to get these guys, Noah. I know that you know how dangerous they are. That's why you came to us."

"I can't just disappear, though."

"It won't be forever." He sighed. "We'll have you disappear in a small town I know. Stay low and you'll be safe. Unless you change your mind about witness protection."

"No, I'm not going forever." I bit my lip. "I don't understand why you can't call Zane and ask him to come in now. We can tell him the plan. He can still help us."

"No." He shook his head. "I can't risk him slipping up. If he thinks you're dead, and he thinks Braydon is responsible, he'll do more. He'll go looking for the truth. We need that."

"You don't know what he'll do."

"We're pretty sure." He smiled at me, tight-lipped, and I looked at the folders on his desk. I saw one with my name and underneath it I saw a label that said "Zane Beaumont." I shivered as I realized that they must have been investigating both of us.

"So what's in the files?" I nodded towards his desk with a frown.

"Everything that exists outside of your minds." He shrugged. "I like to know who I'm dealing with."

"That explains the file about me, but not about Zane."

"What can I say? I had a feeling he was going to be helpful."

"I don't want to go away without telling my brother." I shook my head. "I can't that to him. I can't involve him in something this deep without him knowing the truth."

"You don't have a choice, Noah. Sometimes when you love someone, the best thing you can do is keep them in the dark. Loving someone doesn't always mean telling them everything. It means knowing when it's best to keep your mouth shut and when it's best to open it. And this is the time to keep it shut—that is, if you love your brother as much as you say you do."

"I still want to know about Mom." Zane cleared his throat. "I'm not going to push it right now, but I still want to know." His voice was light.

"You've changed." I cocked my head and studied him. "You're calmer than you were before. I was expecting you to put me in a headlock to get an answer."

"That's coming if you don't give me an answer tomorrow." He grinned at me.

"I'm not keeping it to myself because I want to. Trust me." I made a face. "Just like I didn't leave and not tell you because I wanted to keep you in the dark."

"How could you do it?" He peered at me with hurt eyes. "I would never do that to you. I could never just leave and have you think I'm dead."

"I didn't want to just leave." I sighed. "It's always just been us. I begged to be able to tell you. But Special Agent Waldron convinced me that it was in your best interest for me to not tell you."

"I know you didn't do it to hurt me." He sat on my bed and played with his fingers. "Don't hate me, but I am kind of glad that you didn't tell me. I know it sounds twisted. And I can't believe I'm saying this, but if it wasn't for you going away, I would never have met Lucky. And I don't know what my life would be like if I didn't have her in my life. Do I sound like a complete asshole?" He looked up at me with a twisted smile. "Am I the world's worst brother?"

"No." I laughed lightheartedly. "In fact, it makes you human and very honest."

"I love her so much, you know." He made a face. "It hurts me to be away from her. Like I feel a physical pain. It's crazy."

"That's love. It provides as much joy as it does pain."

"*She* really hurt you, didn't she?"

"Not in the way that you think." I paced in front of the bed. "It's funny, our roles are reversed now. I used to be the one that believed in happy endings, and you were the one with the tortured soul."

"You have a tortured soul? What happened to the rainbows and shit you spouted about when we were growing up?"

"I was living in a daydream. Love isn't always wonderful and flowery. It can be deep, dark, and persevering. It's about accepting the bad with the good. It's about everything we give, get, and forget. We all know the bright side of love as it shines luminously for all to see. But the other side of love, the other side can be a lonely, solitary place. I know that now."

"You ever going to tell me what she did to make you so bitter?"

"Who?" I looked up at him with a bleak smile. "Which she?"

"There's more than one woman who has broken your heart?"

"There's more than one woman who has made me doubt the human race." I walked over to the closet so that Zane couldn't see my face. "But let's not focus on that. I'd rather hear how Lucky has made you believe in love. And then I want to go and hold her tight and ask her if she can introduce me to her God."

"Her God?" Zane's voice sounded confused and I turned around and gave him a smile.

"The God that allowed the two of you to experience the beauty of life and love."

"I'm worried about you, Noah." He jumped up and walked to me slowly before stopping and running his hands through his hair. "You sound like you've turned into Plato or Aristotle or something."

"I prefer to think of myself as Camus." I grinned.

"Camus?"

"Albert Camus." I shook my head. "Oh, big brother of mine. I knew I was smarter than you."

"I can still beat you up, you know." Zane laughed and walked towards the door. "You come talk to me when you're ready to talk." He paused by the door and looked back at me. "About anything. I'm not going to push you about Mom. I've learned how to be patient this last year."

"Thanks." I nodded gratefully. "I will."

"I'll tell Lucky to hold back as well."

"That's okay." I shook my head. "I know she just cares about you. I don't want her to think I'm some sort of asshole. It was really hard, you know, to walk away from you and not be able to tell you. Everything in my life seems to be insignificant up until that point. I just want a fresh start now. I want to start a new life, one that isn't haunted with memories of what has happened since I left."

"I will do what I can to help." He paused and looked back at me. "She cares about you, as well you know. If she asks or holds back, it's because she wants to be a part of your life."

"I know. I wish I'd met her first." I joked, and he came back and punched me lightly in the shoulder.

"I'm glad you didn't." He laughed, his eyes sparkling. "I'm not sure I would have gotten her if I had to compete with you."

"We should go jam." I said, feeling lighthearted. I had missed Zane, really missed him, and I just wanted to be around him and enjoy his company without the pressure of having to have a serious talk.

"You want to?" Zane's eyes looked up and he grinned. "No Beatles, though."

"That's a deal." I nodded and turned my face away from him. A jab of pain shot through me as I remembered always trying to get him to play and listen to The Beatles. It was one of our only links to our mother, and I wanted to remember every little thing about her. I had tried so hard to get Zane to get rid of his bitterness and hurt. As a child, I knew that one day she would come back to us. I had known it in my heart. She loved us more than life itself. What mother doesn't love her sons? Something bad had to have happened for her to desert us.

"That was easy." He looked at me with a question in his eyes. I knew what he wanted to know. He had so many questions and I didn't really have any satisfactory answers. I was in a tough spot, one I didn't know how to get out of. I either kept the truth to myself or told him everything I knew. He would eventually resent me and hate me either way. But I'd rather have him hate me than have him hate himself.

I knew what it was like to hate yourself and I didn't want him to suffer from the same self-inflicted pain that I was. Not if he didn't have to.

CHAPTER FOUR

"*I WISH THAT I COULD SEE you every day.*" *Skylar played with my fingers. "And that we lived in the same house."*

"That would be nice." I nodded and stroked her hair, a feeling of love washing over me. I stared at her face and wondered at the feeling that filled me when I saw her. I'd never experienced

this feeling of protectiveness before. It scared me and I was worried that we were getting too close.

"You could move into my house." She looked up at me hopefully and I shook my head.

"I don't think so." I laughed.

"Why not?"

"Because I have to live in my apartment."

"But you sleep over at my house. You can just always sleep over and never leave."

"I'm not sure that would work out well." I smiled at her sadly. I didn't want to tell her that it was getting harder and harder for me to go over to her house. That in fact, some days I dreaded going over, but I wanted to make sure that she was okay, so I sucked it up.

"One day we can live together." She nodded to herself. *"And you can take care of me."*

"You'd like that would you?" I laughed at her eager expression.

"I'd love that." She jumped up and down. *"I'd be the happiest girl in the world. The very happiest. There would be no other girl in the world as happy as me."*

"Do you want to play a game?" I nodded at the board games on the table. I needed to change the subject. All of a sudden I was overwhelmed with emotion and I couldn't continue the conversation anymore. I felt like I was leading her on to think that her dreams were a possibility. I didn't know how to explain to her that it would never happen. It could never happen. No matter how much I wanted it as well. She had her own family and they were going to make sure that that never happened. They didn't care how much they hurt her. And I couldn't do anything

about it because I'd already revealed too much information. I'd been stupid and said too much and I knew that if I reported what was going on, I would be putting Zane in jeopardy.

"I guess so." She sat back and played with her hair. Her eyes moved away from me and she stared at the floor with a vacant stare. I had no idea what she was thinking about but I had a couple of ideas and it broke my heart to see her in so much pain. But there was nothing I could do to take it away. And that broke my heart into a million pieces.

"Are you nervous?" Lucky turned to me when we pulled into the Johnsons' driveway.

"It does feel like a bit of a first date." I laughed. "I have butterflies in my stomach that are dying to break out."

"I didn't know that guys got nerves as well," she said and then laughed along with me.

"Oh, trust me. We get nerves, all right."

"Are you worried about what they'll say?" Lucky gave me a concerned look. "I'm sure they'll just be happy to see you. And Sidney knew you were not really dead, so he shouldn't be mad at you, right?"

"He won't be mad about that. He won't be mad about anything, really. I know he's disappointed in me for not telling Zane everything about, well, you know, but he's not mad at me. He understands." I jumped out of the car. "Sidney is like a dad to me, a dad and a best friend. It's hard to explain."

"No, I understand. He's a good guy." Lucky nodded. "I'm very fond of him myself."

"I feel like he's a kindred spirit, you know?" I looked into her earnest brown eyes and I could see why my brother loved her so much. "He's been through hell and back in his life and he's not bitter. I want to learn from him. This documentary has served as a learning and educational experience in more ways than one."

"It makes me want to cry when he tells me what he went through." Lucky gave me a weak smile and there were tears in her eyes. "I don't understand how people can hate others that much."

"I think it was fear more than hate." I thought for a moment. "Or fear that simmered and became hate. I don't really understand how people can hurt others, without being affected themselves. It must take a really coldhearted person to hurt someone they should love." My words drifted off as I realized I had gotten off topic.

"Yeah." Lucky looked over at me with questioning eyes. "Hate is a weird emotion. And what it leads people to do. I couldn't even imagine not having access to to school or to teachers. It just seems unfathomable."

"Or being spat upon and tormented mercilessly day by day." I continued her thoughts. "Though it happens today to many children. Too many children are abused mentally, emotionally and physically."

"I know, I guess they are all just bullies." Lucky looked disgusted. "People can be really disgusting sometimes."

"Yes. The targets just change." I sighed and tried to clear my thoughts. Now was not the time for me to start thinking about Palm Bonita. "But let's not dwell on the sad right now. Though you've given me a good idea.

Maybe we can work on a video that talks about the similarities between racism during the times of integration and bullying in schools in modern-day America."

"That's a brilliant idea." Lucky's eyes blazed with excitement. "I hadn't even thought of that, but it sounds like an awesome premise." She reached over and grabbed my hand and squeezed it. "I'm so glad you're back, Noah."

"I am—"

"Are you guys going to stand out on my front lawn the whole day?" Sidney's voice boomed out of the front door, and he grinned at me as I turned towards him.

"Oh, God, Noah." Betty Johnson came out from behind her husband and rushed towards me to give me a hug. "I wouldn't believe it until I saw you with my own two eyes." She held me close to her and I could smell the scent of the after-shower splash she used. I hugged her tightly and gave her a kiss on the cheek.

"I missed you, Betty."

"For shame, boy." She shook her head and slapped my upper arm. "You had all of us so worried and upset." Her words were tight, but I could see the love shining through her eyes as she gazed at me.

"I'm sorry." I bent my head in shame. "You know that I didn't want to hurt anyone."

"I know, now come in and have some tea and cookies." Betty grabbed my arm and led me to the door. "And Lucky, dear, as always it's a pleasure to see you. You're looking positively radiant. I'm so excited for you and Zane. When Sidney told me that he finally came to his senses and proposed, I praised the Lord. Even though, I still think you would be perfect for our Noah."

"Betty!" Sidney admonished her and I laughed easily.

"I agree, Betty. Lucky is the second-most perfect girl for me, after you. Unfortunately, you're both taken."

"Oh, Noah. Ssshhhh." She shook her head but I could see the small smile on her face, showing me that she was happy at my words.

"You sweet talking my wife, boy?" Sidney patted me on the back and his eyes sparkled at me. "You do know she's a married woman?"

"I can't help it if she leaves you for me." I grinned back at him, and my heart filled with affection for him as he gave me a wicked smile.

"Take her, you'll be doing me a favor."

"I'm sure Zane would feel the same way." Lucky laughed. "He'd be only too happy to give me away."

"That boy would kill Noah if he laid a hand on you." Sidney growled. "I just got my boy back. I'm not ready to lose him again so quickly."

"Ha ha. Neither am I." Lucky squeezed my arm before following Betty into the kitchen. "I'll leave you two alone for a bit and go and help Betty in the kitchen."

"So, it's good to see you." Sidney gave me a big hug and studied my face. "You look different." He nodded as if agreeing to a comment someone had made. "You look like a man who has been to the edge of the world and back."

"Really?" I half-smiled. "Though I do feel like I've been to the edge of hell."

"I've missed you." He sat down on a couch, gripping the arms, and my heart sank as I realized how much thinner he looked. His hair was also completely gray, and as I stared at him, it struck me that he had aged significantly. I felt sad that I had missed a year of his life—a year was such a long amount of time.

"I missed you as well. Thank you for keeping my secret."

"It was hard. I'm not going to lie. Your brother looked like death warmed up. If it wasn't for Lucky being there for him, I'm not sure I would have been able to have kept it a secret."

"I would have understood if you had felt the need to tell him. It wasn't fair to burden you like that."

"I was honored that you trusted me enough to tell me."

"You're one of my best friends." I spoke honestly. "I thought about you a lot when I was away."

"So how was it in Palm Beach?" Sidney gave me a wide smile and his eyes danced with mirth.

"You know, I wish I had been in Palm Beach." I laughed. "And you're going to keep at it until I tell you where I was, huh? I was in a city called Palm Bonita, and trust me, Palm Bonita was not a city that would have been featured on *Lifestyles of the Rich & Famous*." I shuddered in remembrance. "Though it may have been the set for the *Twilight Zone*."

"That great?" He shook his head and smiled before his expression turned more serious. He looked me and up and down slowly and then spoke again. "I can tell it was tough. Your eyes tell a different story now."

"They do?" I looked at him in surprise. "I didn't know that my eyes told a story, period," I said and then laughed.

"Yes." Sidney sat back and stretched his legs out carefully. "When we first met, your eyes were full of hope, wonder and sadness. Though the sadness was for me and my story. You were sensitive to what I had been through. You were full of compassion and sincerity, but it was for my story. Now that sadness shines through you as if it has also touched your soul. Your eyes have a tinge of bleakness as well, as if your heart has been cracked a little bit. You're sad now. You've seen other sadness, I think, and this sadness has impacted your life."

He squinted at me, and was silent for a moment as he assessed my face again.

"Wow, you're good." I said slightly uncomfortable at how easily he had been able to read me. I looked to the side of the room and studied the family photographs on the table. "You never told me you were a psychic."

"I've gone through unspeakable pain. I don't talk about it much because the past is the past, but real pain. Gut wrenching pain, it never leaves you. And once you've been through it, you can tell when someone else has." His voice was light, but intense. "Did you know that when I was fifteen, my brother dated a white girl? A pretty young blonde girl. She was a nice girl. Very sweet. They used to go to the movies. Well, one day some neighborhood boys from her school found out and they told my brother to stay away from her. My brother, he didn't listen. We were in the North, you know. We didn't think we had to worry like in the South. In the South, we wouldn't have even looked at a white girl. Well, those boys, they didn't like my brother's answer. One night after he walked Ellen, that was her name, home, he got jumped by about five boys. Beat him black and blue. His nose was bleeding, his lip was cracked, and we come to find out later that he had a few cracked ribs. Well, my brother didn't want to make no fuss. He didn't want to get anyone into any trouble. We found out later that Ellen's brother was involved in the jumping."

"Oh, I'm sorry. That's awful."

"My brother lost sight in his left eye, and Ellen went on to marry one of the boys that beat my brother up." Sidney's voice was sad. "I never could understand how people could be so hateful and vile. That was the incident that broke my trust in humans and their innate goodness. People ain't all good. That's what you got to understand. Some people are just evil. There is no reason to it. It'll break your heart once you realize that. You've realized that now. You've witnessed the cruelty that exists in some human beings. I can see it in your soul."

"I have." I nodded slowly and realized how aptly he had voiced the pain I know felt. Once again I was blown away by how accurate Sidney was in his evaluation of me and his ability to see into my soul and heart. "You're good."

"I wish I wasn't." He smiled at me sadly. "If there was one person I wished would never experience the cruelty of humans to one another, it would be you, my son. You more than anyone shouldn't have to feel and witness the evil in the world. For you are all light, my boy. You were the one that made me believe in goodness again."

"And I'm a good ol' white boy." I grinned at him, touched by his words and he laughed.

"Ain't nothing about color. There be good white men and good black men. And there be bad white men and bad black men. It's about the person inside. Can't judge on the exterior." He looked me in the eyes. "But I know you know that."

"I wish everyone did."

"It comes to most of us sooner or later." Sidney shrugged. "To some it comes on the deathbed. But it comes. I'm lucky I met you. Or I could have spent the rest of my days thinking that all white men be the devil."

"Or the devil incarnate." I grinned at him, and he chuckled.

"So tell me what got you looking like your whole world ended."

"I don't look that bad, do I?" I made a face, and he shook his head.

"To most of the world, I'm sure you look just fine. Maybe better than fine. But to those of us who love you, you look lost."

"I met someone in Palm Bonita." I made a face. "Crazy, right? She was beautiful and sassy and we started dating and at first everything was perfect."

"What changed?"

"She wasn't the person I thought she was."

"She broke your heart?"

"Yeah." I nodded. "Not in the way that you think, though." I sighed and bit my lip before continuing. "I've never really been in love. Or I should say, felt love. I've always had Zane and loved him, but I've never had another person reach that spot in my heart. And in Palm Bonita that changed. I felt an overwhelming and heart-stopping love, and I had to walk away from it, and I'm crushed. And there was nothing I could do. I've never felt so hopeless."

"There's nothing you can do?"

"Not legally."

"That's why you wanted me to contact my son, huh? You've got a big heart." Sidney stared at me, and he looked thoughtful. I had a feeling he understood my vague comments better than I did. It was uncanny how he always seemed to understand what I was thinking or saying without me being very clear.

"Big hearts don't always get you everywhere."

"Everyone's not perfect, Noah." He leaned towards me. "And not everyone has a big heart. You're the exception and not the rule, even though I wish that wasn't true." He paused, and gave me a look. "But you're not God, Noah. You can't protect everyone."

"You want me to tell Zane." I sighed.

"He has a right to know. You can't just hide that from him."

"You just don't understand. I think he'll be devastated if he learns the truth. Growing up, he had so many issues and so much hatred towards our mom. And I just don't want to see him go through any more unnecessary pain."

"You can't not tell him because you're afraid of how it will affect him. He's a big boy."

"I don't want him to feel any differently about me, either." I made a face. "I know I'm being selfish, but I don't want our relationship to change."

"It's not your fault, Noah. He's not going to blame you."

"It changes everything."

"It changes nothing."

"It's a life-changing piece of information." I took a deep breath.

"Have you spoken to your mom?"

"No." I shook my head. "I can't respect her for what she did."

"Can't you forgive her?"

"She wants nothing to do with Zane." I almost whispered the words. "I don't know how she can distance herself like that."

"Love is a funny thing."

"I can't accept it." I shook my head vehemently. "I've witnessed first-hand the devastation that comes from not being wanted."

"It's a cruel thing to do to a child."

"I won't lose two people to that sort of devastation. I don't want be a witness to two people being heartbroken from the pain and rejection of two people that should love them." I jumped up as I saw Lucky and Betty approaching the door. "Need any help, ladies?"

"We're fine, thank you." Lucky smiled at me gratefully as she walked into the room. She placed the teapot on the table and Betty followed behind her with a tray of cups and saucers. She gasped quickly and rubbed her belly in amazement and I stared at her with a worried expression.

"Is everything okay?"

"Yes, it's great. I think I just felt the babies kick for the first time. Come." She motioned me over to her and grabbed my hand and placed it on her stomach. "Let's see if they do it again." I stood there waiting for a few moments, but nothing happened. I let go of her stomach, slightly disappointed, and Sidney gave me a look.

"It's a good thing them babies didn't kick again, you know how disappointed their papa would have been if he would have heard that news."

"He'd kill me." I laughed. "After everything that has happened, this would be the straw that broke the camel's back."

"You don't want to break the camel's back." Betty poured the tea and handed me a cup. "Not when the camel just started walking again."

"Zane's not that crazy." Lucky shook her head at the offer of a teacup. "I'll just have water, thanks, Betty."

"He's not. But it's a special moment. I'm sure he'd like to be the first to feel his babies kick."

"Yeah." Lucky blushed. "About that, I think I was mistaken." She giggled. "I think I had gas."

"Really?" I laughed as a tide of red covered her face.

"Yeah." She nodded. "I think it's too early for the babies to be kicking. I'll have to check with the doctor. I'm pretty sure what I felt wasn't a kick." She groaned.

"Do not tell Zane, please. He'll never let me live this down."

"Okay." I smiled at her and ruffled her hair. "You owe me one."

"Now, children, are we going to talk about our documentary? Are all systems go now?" Sidney interrupted us and raised an eyebrow at me. "I've told my whole family about this film, and everyone in Chicago is waiting to see my ugly mug on the screen."

"You're not ugly, Sidney," Lucky protested while Betty rolled her eyes.

"Don't play into his act, Lucky." She sat down next to me and handed me a plate with an assortment of cookies. I took a piece of shortbread and she nodded at me encouragingly to take another piece. "You're a growing boy, Noah. Another piece of shortbread won't stay on your hips like it does mine."

"What about me?" Sidney frowned and leaned forward to grab a cookie.

"You don't need any cookies." Betty glared at him. "Think of your cholesterol. You know what Dr. Rothstein said."

"Dr. Rothstein doesn't know everything." Sidney sat back and looked at me with a 'Well, this sucks' face.

"He knows more than you do." Betty scolded him. "And he told you to stay away from cookies, cakes, fried dishes—"

"Yeah, yeah." He turned towards me. "So, I was thinking that it would be cool if you featured my other wife as well."

"Excuse me?" I looked at him in confusion.

"I thought you could include my other wife in the documentary."

"What other wife?" I looked at Betty, who was mumbling under her breath.

"The one I'm going to marry once I divorce Betty for not allowing me to eat the things I enjoy." Sidney laughed, and Betty shook her head at him.

"I swear, Sidney Johnson, you're just like a little boy."

"Well, what do you expect if you keep mothering me?" He rolled his eyes.

"I wouldn't mother you if you acted your age and listened to the doctor."

"Doctors don't always get it right. Didn't I tell you how they cut off Louis's right leg instead of his left because the doctor read the chart wrong? Now instead of only having one leg, he has none. And whose fault was that?" Sidney's voice rose. "Not Louis's, I'll tell you that."

"Well, it was Louis's fault that he let his diabetes get so bad that he needed to have any leg cut off." Betty responded back to him with a stern look, and Lucky and I exchanged a quick smile at their banter. I decided to interrupt the conversation because I had a feeling that it was only going to escalate if I didn't.

"So, I was thinking that the focus of the documentary could be about identity." I paused and realized that everyone was staring at me in interest. "Originally, the focus of this documentary was going to be on race and the civil rights movement, but I've been thinking and I want to expand our subject matter. Let's be honest, our current audience is limited. Race is a sensitive subject, and not everyone can relate. Or, let's be honest, not everyone wants to relate. I want people to understand that we're all in this together. We all have issues related to poverty and identity and we've all faced them in different ways."

"You haven't really had poverty issues though." Lucky looked at me seriously. "And I don't want to dumb down the documentary because it might make people uncomfortable. Let's be real here, African Americans have had the worst assimilation experience in the United States."

"But that doesn't mean that others don't also have their own issues. As humans, we inherently care about other people. It's in our nature. But we care more about what affects us in our everyday lives, and our families. So if we can create a piece that talks about the very real experiences that people have gone through related to identity, then we can reach more people."

"I guess I don't understand. What identity issues are you talking about? I know you're not going to talk about the issues of being a white male." Lucky made a face and her voice was loud and obstinate. "Because we all know that the best thing to be in life is a white male."

"Some would say a white female." I cocked my head and stared at her. "Doesn't she control the white male?"

"Women as a whole are seen as inferior to men." Lucky's voice grew agitated. "We're seen as sex objects or domesticators. Men do not take us seriously. Not as a whole. And not every white female has power. What about the women that aren't as attractive, or who grow up in poor environments, or what about those who are lesbians?"

"Exactly my point. There are many denominators in everyone's story. Yes, it's true. You take a random white male and a random black male and it is very likely that the white male has had more advantage in his life. But it's not true for everyone. To be born white and male doesn't guarantee anything in life. To be born white, male, and with the last name Kennedy or Windsor may mean something else. But most of us don't fit that mold."

"I don't want to focus a historical documentary on the plight of white males." Lucky looked at me with disappointment, and I held my hand up.

"I think you're misunderstanding me." I looked at Sidney and Betty, who were both looking at me with interested looks on their faces. I smiled at them gratefully, glad that they didn't look as upset as Lucky did at my suggestion.

"Here's the thing. I don't want the focus to be about black or white. I want the focus to be on this. This is the trajectory of life for certain people. I don't want to tell people this is the story of every black American, or the story of every white American. I want people to think, 'Wow, this is a powerful story, and this is how it connects to my life.' I want people to look at their everyday lives and realize how much they have in common with people that they would never think they had anything in common with. I don't want this to be a black story about black people. I don't want people to say, 'Well, segregation is over, and that was the past. We're past that now.' It's not true. And it's not fair. I want people to see that this is a story about human beings and that our identities are made up of things that don't matter. Our race doesn't matter, our gender doesn't matter, our bloodlines don't matter. We should love and treat each other equally. At the end of the day, we need to see past these things. We need to understand that love, true love, the love that we should feel for each other isn't or shouldn't be based on things beyond our control." My voice was loud and incensed as I finished talking and I sat back slightly embarrassed at how passionate I had gotten as I was talking. "Sorry, you guys can disagree with me. I just wanted to tell you my thoughts."

"I like your ideas." Lucky grinned at me. "I think you're right. We'll reach a wider audience, and we won't alienate as many people."

"Thanks." I turned towards Sidney and Betty to see what they thought. I held my breath as I was slightly worried that they were going to be upset with me. I looked at Betty first and she gave me a warm smile. Her eyes shone at me with emotion and she patted my knee as if consoling me for the hidden feelings that she knew were trying to escape.

"You've grown." Sidney's voice was serious and low. "I remember the boy that walked through my front door, so incensed about the injustice that I had been through, that many blacks have been through. The boy who felt my pain but didn't quite understand the dynamics of that history. And now you're a man, and you've got your own story, one that you want to tell, and I'm hurting for you inside. But behind that hurt is pride. I'm proud of you, my son. I'm proud of the man you're becoming. I was proud of the boy you were. But I'm proud of the man you are becoming as well. Just don't let what you've gone through break you. We love you, and we are all here for you when you're ready to talk about it." Sidney sat up slowly. "And I'll tell you all one thing, one thing that hits home in this whole conversation. My life changed the day I stopped looking at myself as a black man first and foremost. I look at myself as a man and a husband. My race, as categorized through the eyes of others, doesn't make up who I am. If someone chooses to be afraid of me, or to look down upon me, or think I'm uneducated, or inferior, well, that's on them. That's between them and their God. I don't take on those stereotypes anymore. I'm not a criminal and I'm not inferior. I'm black and I'm God damn proud of it, but that doesn't define my life. I won't let that fear of what others are thinking or feeling about me control me. It's taken me a long time to get to this place. My identity has always been that of a black man and what that means for me and for everyone around me. Now my identity is that of a loving husband and father." He laughed. "Don't get it wrong, though. I've only recently gotten to that place. But I've been angry and upset for too long now. I realized that God didn't want me to carry that burden any longer."

"That's not an easy thing to do." My stomach twisted as I thought about Skylar and the burden I carried around with me every day.

"It's not easy, but sometimes letting go and forgiving others and yourself is the only way to move forward in life." Sidney stared into my eyes. "There's always more life to live, and sometimes you just have to live it. You don't want to wake up and be eighty years old and regretting the path you took."

"Yeah." I nodded and looked down. "It's just not that easy to move on. Especially when you know the other person is still living in that place, in that pain, and there is nothing you can do to stop it."

"There's never nothing you can do." Sidney looked up and stared at me. "You just have to think it through a little bit harder. But there's never nothing you can do."

"That's true." I nodded at him and sighed. There was one thing I could do, but if I did it, there was a possibility I could go to jail for the rest of my life. And even worse than that was the possibility that I could put Skylar in even more harm.

CHAPTER FIVE

"*A*REN'T YOU GOING TO KISS ME?"
She grinned up at me, with a devilish glint in
her blue eyes. "We've been on two dates now."

"I didn't want to assume anything." I smiled at her and
studied her pouty bright red lips. "Though I suppose I should have
read the signs a bit better."

"The signs?"

"Your hooker red lipstick." I laughed and stared at her
pouty bright red lips.

"Hooker red?" She leaned in closer to me and ran her fingers down my chest.

"Not that I'm calling you a hooker."

"Of course not." She pressed her breasts against my chest lightly. "You'd be paying me if I was a hooker, and I would be demanding payment upfront."

"Payment upfront, huh?" I laughed. "Are you trying to take me for all my money?"

"It depends on how much money you have." She whispered against my lips. "I'm still waiting, by the way."

"I suppose if you want a kiss, I shouldn't disappoint you."

"I don't suggest that at all." Her arms encircled my waist and she pulled me towards her. I felt the bulge in my pants hardening against her stomach, and I guess she felt it as well because I saw her grin and lick her lips.

"Hopefully the kiss doesn't disappoint you, though," I teased her before leaning down and tracing my tongue along her lower lip, before sinking my teeth into it.

"I don't think you'll disappoint me." She breathed out huskily before raising her hands to my face and running her hands through my hair. "Not at all." She breathed against my lips before reaching up and pressing her breasts against my chest and kissing me passionately. Her tongue was in my mouth before I even knew what was happening, and she tasted like a minty, mysterious paradise. I kissed her back with fervor, nibbling on her tongue as my hands explored her back. I felt her hands reach under my shirt, and she scratched my back as she sunk into me. My hands found their way to the front of her top, and I gently caressed her stomach as my fingers worked their way up to her bra. She gasped as I gently squeezed her nipple, and I felt her fingers work their way to my belt, which she promptly unbuckled. Her lips encircled my tongue and sucked tightly as her fingers encircled my now extremely hard erection. I pulled her towards me tightly as I felt the thrill of sex coursing through my body. My fingers slipped up under her bra, and I felt her body melting into mine as they traced the curve of her breast.

"Come back inside." She purred as she looked up at me.

"Are you sure?" I held her arms up and pressed her against the door, so she could feel the full length of my hardness against her.

"I want you inside of me, so yes, I'm sure." She licked her lips slowly and seductively.

"I see." I laughed, suddenly feeling a bit like a fish out of water.

"I don't play games, Noah. I know what I want and I want you." Her face hardened a little bit. *"The question is, are you up for it?"*

"I'm always up for it." I growled back at her, not liking how she was challenging my masculinity. There was something about her that put me on edge. I was attracted and intrigued by her, but a part of me didn't even like her.

"Then come inside." She grabbed my arm and pulled me back into the apartment. *"I told you to be careful of the big bad wolf."*

"I'm no piggy." I stared back at her. *"You're not going to blow my house down."*

"I wouldn't be too sure of that." She laughed as she drew me into her bedroom and pulled her top off. I stared at her as she casually slipped her bra off and flung it into my face. *"Don't play with fire unless you're prepared to be burned."* She fell back on the bed and stared up at me through veiled eyes. I ignored her words and jumped onto the bed, yanking my shirt off and throwing it on the ground. She grabbed a hold of me and pushed me onto my back, before pulling my pants and hers off in a quick movement. Her mouth was bobbing up and down on my erection within moments and I grunted as I pulled her hair, not feeling anything but the

wanton pull of a near-orgasm. My eyes popped open as I heard the sound of footsteps, and I gasped as I saw the eyes of someone watching us through the doorway.

"Wait." I pulled her away from me in a panic. "I think I just saw someone."

"Oh." She looked at me in surprise. "Don't worry about it."

"Are you sure?" I frowned at her. "There was someone watching us."

"She's a freak." She shrugged before going back down on me. "I'll be rid of her soon."

"Who is—" I started but stopped as I felt myself coming close to a climax. I lay back on the bed, enjoying the sweet feeling of my release, but I couldn't stop the uncomfortable feeling that was spreading through my body. Who was the girl who had been watching us through the door, and why was I feeling as if I was making the biggest mistake of my life?

Running helps me to clear my mind. I like to run for miles and miles and jam to hip hop music while I think through whatever is on my mind. Many people run to lose weight or to train for a marathon to raise money for some good cause. I run for me. I run to clear my mind from all my unanswered questions. I run to speak to God. I'm not sure when I started having conversations with Him. I've never been particularly religious. I didn't grow up going to church or reading the Bible. I couldn't tell you the names of the apostles or the gospels, but somehow I had developed a relationship with God. I think my conversations started my first night in Palm Bonita. And while I never heard a voice speaking back to me, I did always feel like I had been heard after my runs. I couldn't stop thinking about what Sidney had said to me yesterday. I knew, in my heart of hearts, that I needed to stop letting the guilt weigh me down. But it consumed me when the lights went out and I was alone in my bed, all alone. All I could think about was Skylar and the look in her eyes when she realized that I wasn't her savior. She had begged me to take her away from Palm Bonita, and I had said no. She didn't know that I had tried. That I had wracked my brain trying to think of a way to save her from the life she found herself in. She'd cried. Big tears filled with sadness and fear. I could still see the look in her eyes when we'd had that last conversation. It was exactly the same as the first time I had seen her. That haunted wide-eyed look was imprinted in my mind. Now when I run, my conversations with God are angry ones, and no matter how many miles I run, I still never feel like I've totally cleared my mind.

"Well, hey, there, stalker." A voice cut into my thoughts and I looked to the side in irritation. I was surprised to see a familiar face next to me. It was the snotty girl from the restaurant. I groaned inside as I nodded at her. I really didn't want to deal with the waitress and her issues right now. I also didn't want to think about the spark I felt when I looked in her eyes. "No hello?" She smiled at me teasingly and I gave her a weak smile back.

"I like to run in silence." I spoke finally, and she looked at my earphones with a sharp stare.

"I didn't realize that country music was silent."

"I didn't realize that Jay-Z was a country music star."

"Aha, so you're listening to music." She gave me an 'I got you' stare and I stifled a sigh and increased the pace of my run. She grinned at me and increased her own pace. "Trying to get away from me?"

"Look, I don't know you." I shrugged and frowned at her. "We met once, and frankly you were a bit of a bitch. I'm not sure why you really care to talk to me now." I said harshly, annoyed that I was somewhat happy inside to see her.

"I'm sorry about the other day." She made a face. "I had a bit of an attitude. It had been a long day. Thanks for not telling my manager."

"Yeah." I kept my face straight. "No problem."

"Don't you want to know what happened?"

"Not really."

"Oh." She bit her lower lip and I saw her stare at me uncertainly. "I guess I should let you run by yourself now." Her voice sounded a bit unsure and I realized that she most probably wasn't used to being brushed off by guys. Even among all the hot girls in Los Angeles, a girl as pretty as she was would get a lot of attention.

"See ya around." I nodded and continued running.

"Ow!" she screamed, and I paused to look behind me. She was sprawled on the concrete face down, with scratched palms and a bleeding knee.

"You okay?" I sighed and ran back to help her up.

"I tripped." She stood up slowly and sighed.

"Over?" I looked at the flat surface of the pavement in bewilderment.

"My own two feet." She blushed and looked away. "Thanks for the help, you can continue on your way now." She pulled her hands away from me, and I felt suddenly bereft at the loss of her touch.

"Look, I didn't mean to be rude." I sighed. "It's been a long week."

"It's okay." She smiled at me tightly. "I don't know why I expected you to be friendly to me. Like you said, you don't know me, and the one time we did meet I wasn't exactly nice."

"Yeah, you weren't." I made a face and laughed.

"Sorry about that."

"It's okay." I reached my hand out to her. "Let's start over. I'm Noah, Noah Beaumont."

"Robin." She smiled and shook my hand firmly. "Robin Cartwright."

"Not shrew?"

"What?"

"Nothing but a bad joke." I groaned to myself. "It's nice to meet you again, Robin."

"You too, Noah." She beamed at me, and her brown eyes sparkled. I stared in amazement as they seemed to change colors right before me. Sharing a smile with Robin awakened something in me, and I tried to ignore the stirrings of interest that pervaded my body.

"Are you okay to run, or do you need help to your car or anything?"

"I'm okay." She laughed. "I'm a bit of a klutz. I'll be fine."

"You need to take better care of yourself."

"Yes, Dad." She rolled her eyes and I laughed. I had heard Lucky say something similar to Zane earlier that morning when he had told her to be careful as she was vacuuming the stairs. I guess the paternal instinct was alive and well in both Zane and me.

"I'm not trying to say that you won't take better care of yourself." I tripped over my words as she stood there standing there with her hands on her hips and an amused look in her eyes.

"I'm glad to hear that." She grinned at me and started laughing. "Who knew that a guy as handsome as you could be so awkward?"

"You think I'm handsome?" I smiled at her with a happy smile. A swell of pleasure filled me as I stared at her.

"I also said you're awkward."

"Awkward's cute." I gave her a lop-sided smile and stuck my tongue out. "I don't take offense to awkward. But I do take pleasure in handsome. Handsome is even better than cute. You can't buy handsome. Not even in Beverly Hills."

"You're a dork." She shook her head, laughing at me.

"An awkward, handsome dork." I held my hands up in the air. "I sound like a winner."

"You're incorrigible."

"But I'm still handsome." I grinned at her, all worries gone from my mind. I was enjoying our banter more than I had enjoyed anything in a long while.

Robin rolled her eyes and leaned over and brushed my chest softly. My breath caught at her touch and I stared at her wondering if she had felt the same spark of electricity.

"You had some fluff on your t-shirt." She offered an explanation for her touch and stood back with a slightly bewildered look in her eyes.

"Thanks for brushing it off." *Touch me again.* I wanted to beg her to press her hands against me again. Her touch had ignited something in me. Her fingers had made me feel something deep inside where it was dark and cold. Her touch had created warmth.

"I don't normally do this, but would you like to go for a drink tonight?" She laughed girlishly and lowered her eyes.

"A drink?" I took a step back.

"Yeah, you know. You get a whiskey or a gin and tonic and I get a white Russian or a sex on the beach." She grinned at me effortlessly.

"Sorry." I shook my head. "I've got plans."

"Figures." She smiled ruefully. "All the good guys are gone."

"I'm not dating anyone." My voice sounded harsh and she looked up at me with a curious expression. "Sorry, recent break-up." I softened my tone.

"That's okay. I've been there." She shuddered. "And I've been a lot meaner to you, so no need to apologize."

"Well, I should probably get going." My heart was beating rapidly and my body was starting to feel warm with confusion. "I need to finish my run before I turn into a slob."

"Yeah, you don't want to turn into a slob." Her eyes looked me up and down, and she didn't hide the fact that she was impressed by my muscular frame. I tried to ignore the feelings of pleasure that rose in me again at her obvious interest. I was in no place to start dating.

"Glad you're concerned for me." I started jogging in place. "But I should be going now."

"You got your phone?"

"Yeah, why?"

"Take my number. In case you ever change your mind and want to get that drink." She smiled. "And I'll even buy the first round."

"How can a guy say no to that?" I smiled at her and handed her my phone.

"I don't know. How *can* a guy say no to that?" She grinned at me impishly and then handed me back my phone.

"Only a fool would say no!" I slipped the phone back into my pocket. "And I dare say I am that fool."

"Well, fools can change their ways." She hesitated before continuing. "I hope you don't think I'm being too forward. I just feel really bad about how I acted in the restaurant. I'm new to Los Angeles and I'm the cliché drama student who wants to be an actress and make it big and, well, I'm just trying to meet some new people. And not sleep my way to the top, though it seems that all producers want to do is see how far I'm willing to go on the casting couch." She paused and slapped her hand to her mouth. "Not that you wanted to know any of that." She sighed. "Sorry again. I'm an over-sharer."

"Then you fit into Los Angeles already." I gave her a reassuring smile as I studied her face. I liked her like this, not so confident and slightly out of her element. It made me feel like we had something in common. "We all over-share here. It's a problem we have. It's like we all think our lives are a movie and we want everyone to understand every single part of it. Cue angsty music from Paramore." I laughed and she joined me, while running her hands through her hair.

"You haven't really shared much with me, though." She pursed her lips. "I barely know your name."

"That's because I don't live my life as if it's a movie." I looked to the ground for a moment before looking back up and catching a flicker of remorse on her face. "But really, I should get going. I'll give you a call sometime," I lied to her.

"That would be great." She nodded at me, and looked away. "I'll catch you later, Noah."

"Yeah."

I ran away from her quickly, feeling suddenly alone as I left her. As I got to the corner, I looked back quickly to get one more glimpse of her and I saw her still standing in the same place staring blankly at the space in front of her. My heart panged for her as I wondered what she was thinking about. Part of me wanted to run back to her and find out what was going on in her life. I wanted to know where she grew up, where she had gone to college, why she wanted to be an actress, what sort of actress she wanted to be. I wanted to tell her that she was so much more than just the cliché drama student who comes to L.A. to make it big. She had charisma and character. She was someone that you didn't forget easily. She was someone I wasn't going to forget easily. Even though I barely knew her.

But instead I continued running away from her. I couldn't help her or save her. It wasn't fair to bring her into the confusion in my life. Not when I still had so much unresolved. Not when my heart still had a hole in it the size of the Mississippi. I thought back to what Sidney had said about moving on in life and making a fresh start. But a part of me didn't want to forget. A part of me still hoped that everything could still work out. And while I still had hope, it wasn't fair to bring someone else into my life. No matter how many times my stomach flipped just thinking about her.

CHAPTER SIX

"*I* JUST WANT IT TO BE *us, Noah. I know you love Zane and he means something to me. But I just want it to be us. You can move here, to France, and we can make up for all the years we've lost.*" *She stroked the side of my face as she looked at me with wide eyes.*

"I can't do that." I shook my head, trying hard to keep my anger in.

"Be a good boy for your mama."

"You gave up the right to that title the day you walked away from me and Zane."

"I already explained that to you, Noah. Your papa almost broke me. I had to get away." Her breath caught. "I've thought about you every day since I've been gone."

"How can you have stopped loving him?" I studied her face bitterly. "What sort of person are you?"

"The connection just wasn't—"

"You used to take him out. Just him." I interrupted her accusingly. "You even asked him to look after me."

"He was always a strong-willed and protective boy. I knew that he would grow up to be an assertive man. I wanted to make sure that you were taken care of."

"Most people are taken care of by their parents."

"Your dad never loved me." She grabbed my hands and looked at me with pleading eyes. "I couldn't take it. I wanted to take you with me, but I knew he wouldn't let me."

"But what about Zane? Didn't you love him as well?"

"In my own way." She looked at me sorrowfully, her eyes begging me to understand.

"I can't believe that you don't love your own son."

"He was never my son."

"I'm getting fed up of waiting around, Lucky." Zane's voice was loud as I slipped in the front door. I could hear his voice booming from the kitchen and I paused, not wanting to interrupt what sounded like a tense moment.

"Patience is a virtue." Lucky's voice was softer but I could tell that she felt for him. "Give him time."

"It's hard. I just want to know. Why wouldn't he tell me?" He sounded frustrated. "I'm not trying to be an asshole. I want to understand. I mean, I do understand that he thinks he's protecting me, but shit, I want to know what the fuck is going on. She's my mom as well. He can't just keep this shit to himself."

"It's obviously important to him." Lucky paused. "I'm worried about him, Zane. Last week when we were at the Johnsons', he seemed really sad and alone. I know you don't think we should try and introduce him to anyone, but I think he needs to get out there. I know he's your brother and you love him, and I know you're frustrated and you want answers, but maybe you should think about how this has affected him. It's been hard for you, yes, very hard. But you have me now. But what does

Noah have? Who does Noah have? He's carrying all these burdens all by himself. It can't be easy for him." Lucky's voice cracked. "I'm actually really worried about him." Her voice went low, and I couldn't hear what she was saying.

I leaned against the front door and frowned to myself. They were worried about me, and Zane was getting irritable, which I had expected. He had never been especially patient when we were growing up and frankly, I was surprised that he hadn't threatened me for more information already. But it was Lucky who had broken my heart. Hearing the worry and despair in her voice as she spoke about me concerned me. I didn't want her feeling sorry for me or worrying about me. I knew it wasn't safe for her to be stressed during her pregnancy. I knew I hadn't been doing a great job of hiding my emotions or my semi-depression, but I didn't realize I'd been doing as shitty a job as I had been. I knew that I had to do something to make them think I was moving on in my life. I grabbed my phone and slowly exited the house to make a call.

"Hello?" Her voice was soft and questioning.

"Hey, it's Noah."

"Hey."

"The guy you met in the restaurant and jogging the other—"

"I know who you are." She laughed. "What's up?"

"You didn't hang up." I grinned into the phone.

"Were you expecting me to?" She laughed. "I know I was a bit of a bitch the first day we met, but I did give you my number. Not the other way around."

"So I was wondering … would you like to come over for dinner one night?" The words ran out of my mouth before I could stop them.

"Is that code for 'come over and have sex'?"

"No, no. Sorry, I meant come over and have dinner with my brother, his fiancée and myself."

"A meet and greet on the first date."

"Well, it's not a date. I mean, argh." I groaned into the phone. "Sorry, I kind of suck at this."

"You do suck a lot more than I thought you would."

"I hope that's not bad."

"Were you in a long relationship or something?"

"Not really. But I've been in some bad ones." I sighed and changed the subject. "But you don't want to talk about that."

"Yeah, we haven't even been on a date yet. I don't want the past relationship talk already."

"So would you like to come over? For dinner, I mean. Nothing else." I cleared my throat and shook my head at myself. "I mean, it's not a booty call or anything. Not that you're not good enough for a booty call. I'm just not using you as a booty call. But this is just a friendly get-together."

"I knew you were awkward." She laughed. "I just didn't realize how awkward."

"I'm honestly really not this bad." I paced back and forth, enjoying our conversation. "I think you just bring out the teenage boy in me."

"Were you a skinny nerdy teenager?" She laughed. "And you transformed into a muscular hunk?"

"Not really." I laughed. "I've always been a bit of a hunk."

"That's what I figured. So why so awkward with me?"

"Maybe it's because you're special." I answered honestly and Robin fell silent. "I didn't mean special special, just that you're a good person."

"We shouldn't do this." She spoke thoughtfully and slowly. "It's not a good idea."

"What's not a good idea?" I was worried and slightly angry at her words. "It's just a dinner."

"It's never just a dinner." She sighed. "You seem like trouble, Noah Beaumont. I don't need any more trouble in my life."

"I just want to be friends." I spoke hurriedly into the phone, feeling slightly panicked. What if she decided not to come to dinner? I hadn't considered that possibility.

"I don't think you know what you want." She paused. "There's nothing wrong with that. I just don't know that I can be the person that helps you figure it out."

"There's nothing to figure out." I gripped the phone tightly. "Please come to dinner. It will be fun."

"Do you have a girlfriend?"

"No! Of course not." I shook my head vehemently and then stopped when I realized she couldn't see me.

"Did you break up with her or did she break up with you?"

"It was mutual." My voice was pained as I spoke. I didn't want to relive the memories of my time in Palm Bonita with her.

"Do you still care about her?" She paused. "Stupid question. I can already tell that you do."

"What?" I frowned. "What are you talking about?"

"It's okay if you think I'm crazy and intense." She spoke into the phone hurriedly. "I suppose I am a little bit. Along with being a bitch and slightly neurotic. And a game show fiend. But I can't get into a relationship or dating situation with someone who is caught up with their ex."

"I just called to ask you for dinner." I couldn't stop myself from laughing. "Not to get married."

"I guess it would be nice to make some new friends," she said slowly. "If you're sure you don't mind having a friend who could be in the loony bin."

"You'll fit right in." I smiled, suddenly happy that we were back on track. "Can you make it tonight?"

"Tonight?" She sounded surprised. "I'm not sure."

"Please?" I closed my eyes and pictured her face. "It would be nice to see you again," I said honestly.

"Well, since you ask that nicely," she laughed, "I'd love to."

"Great. Shall I pick you up?"

"I can make my way to you. Where do you live?"

"Los Feliz."

"Oh, fancy."

"What about you?"

"Los Feliz as well."

"Oh, well, I guess you're fancy, too."

"I'm not sure you could call the apartment complex I live in fancy. Maybe a fancy dump."

"Well, I live with my brother, and so while his place isn't a dump, I can't claim it as my own."

"I look forward to seeing it."

"I look forward to seeing you." I almost whispered into the phone, lightheaded. I was amazed that I was really enjoying the conversation and was anxious to see her again. I hadn't thought that I could feel so into someone new with the other worries in my mind. A part of me was ashamed that I was allowing light and happiness into my life while Skylar was still stuck in the dark. I shook my head to stop the sad thoughts from creeping in and taking over.

"Well, if you're a good boy, you may even get a goodnight kiss," she teased me happily.

"Then I'll have to be very good."

"Noah?" Zane opened the front door and stared at me on the phone. "I thought I heard someone outside. You okay?"

"Yeah." I nodded. "I'll be right in. I'm on the phone."

He looked at me with an almost accusatory stare and I suddenly realized that he thought I was on the phone with Mom. "A new friend of mine is coming over to dinner tonight. We're just making plans," I explained to him, and the wariness in his eyes faded.

"Oh, okay." He stepped back. "I'll be in the kitchen."

"See you in a minute." I waited for him to go back in before continuing. "Sorry about that, Robin, my brother came outside."

"That's okay. I should get going anyway. Text me your address and what time to be there and I'll see you later tonight."

"Sounds good."

"Shall I bring anything?"

"Just yourself."

I stood outside for a few minutes after we got off the phone to gather my thoughts. I had initially called Robin to soothe Lucky's fears and worries, but I was genuinely excited for her to come to dinner. More excited than I should be, but I wasn't really surprised. I had been attracted to her the first time I'd seen her. And now that I was getting to know her, I was even more drawn to her. I liked her honesty and wit. I liked the way she challenged me and wasn't afraid to say what she felt. She didn't seem like she was a girl who was into games. What you saw was what you got. And she seemed like a good person. My heart thudded as I thought about Robin and the feelings that were already developing in me. I was scared. I had been wrong once before. I had allowed sex to manipulate my mind and now I was paying the ultimate price. "They're not the same." I muttered to myself. I didn't want to compare them, but I was already doubting my instincts. What did I really know about Robin? Was I allowing sex to guide me again? I had gotten it wrong before. Very wrong. And now I didn't know what to think. As I stood there, I thought back to the moment in Palm Bonita when I had realized that maybe she was the bad news she had been warning me about all along.

"You coming?" She'd grabbed my hand and pulled me into the small room besides her. "I don't think this is a good idea." I mumbled but followed her in. "Let's go." I watched as she went through the drawers and pulled out items of clothing and stuffed them into her bag. "Let's go." I said louder this time, hoping she

sensed my displeasure and the urgency with which I wanted to leave. "This isn't cool."

"You thought it was cool when you thought we were going to have sex in here." She rolled her eyes at me. "So you're fine with having sex in a stranger's house, but not borrowing stuff?"

"You're not borrowing anything. You're stealing." I grabbed her arm and pulled her toward me. "I thought it would be kind of kinky to make love in a stranger's house, I admit it. But it was a bad idea. Let's go."

"Hold on, let me see what she has in the closet first." She pulled away from me, and her voice was harsh. "I heard she had a Chanel handbag in here somewhere." She threw clothes on the ground and then I heard her take a sharp breath as she stuffed something in her bag. "Louis Vuitton will do." She turned towards me with a seductive glance. "Now, if you want to get laid, I'm all yours." I watched her in horror and lust as she pulled her top off and then pulled her bra off as she walked towards me. "Take me, Noah."

"No, no. I can't." I resisted the urge to grab her and bend her over.

"You know you want to." She pressed her lips against mine aggressively and I pulled away in distaste.

"No. Let's go."

"Fuck me, asshole, or I'll tell Mr. and Mrs. Braithwaite that you broke in."

"What?" I looked at her in disbelief.

"I'm joking." She stepped back and slipped her shirt back on. "Let's go." And then we walked out of the back door, just as easily as we had entered. "What do you want to do now?"

"I think I'm just going to go home." I walked away from her without looking her in the eyes. I felt disgusted with myself, and I couldn't stop the churning feeling of horror that was seeping into my veins. What we had done hadn't been sexy or fun. It had been invasive and creepy. Who was I becoming? This wasn't who I was. But now I was starting to wonder who she was.

"Noah," she called after me and I turned to look at her slowly, trying to ignore the mixed feelings that rushed through me at her face. "Remember what I said before." She looked at me coldly as she held a finger up to her lips. I turned away from her and walked away quickly with my heart pounding. I didn't know what to think or say but all of a sudden I wanted to be anywhere but in Palm Bonita. That night I had insomnia and all I could think of was how disappointed Zane would be with me. And so I went to my stash of cash and slipped $5,000 in an envelope and *left it in the Braithwaites' mailbox. Giving them the cash helped to assuage some of my guilt, but I still felt uneasy. That was the day that I realized that she had an evil side. And I was scared that I had gotten her all wrong.*

"You coming in, Noah?" Lucky opened the door and peeked out at me with a smile.

"Yeah, sorry. Just got distracted."

"So what's this I hear about a dinner date?" Her voice was excited and happy, and I knew that at least I had gotten one thing right.

"Remember that waitress at the restaurant?"

"The one that didn't like you?"

"Yeah," I laughed. "Well she's coming over to dinner tonight."

"Tonight!" Her jaw fell open and I could see a million questions in her eyes. "Come inside, we need to decide what to cook."

"I'm sure whatever you make will be good." I followed her inside and into the kitchen.

"Whatever I decide to cook?" She laughed and shook her head. "You Beaumont brothers are really incorrigible." She slipped her arm through mine and smiled up at me. "There is no way I'm cooking the whole dinner tonight. But I'll help."

"Please, Lucky." I gave her a pleading smile and she shook her head.

"Nope. Anyways, it will be more romantic if you cook most of it. Right, Zane?" She looked over at him and he rolled his eyes.

"I have no clue." He shrugged. "I don't care who cooks the food as long as it tastes good."

"Zane." Lucky frowned at him. "So I guess you don't want me to cook anymore."

"No, no, no. That's not what I meant," he backtracked quickly and I chuckled.

"Now, now, children. No need to bicker." I looked down at Lucky and saw the mirth in her eyes as she beamed up at me.

"What about steak?"

"That sounds good."

"Is she vegetarian, though?" She suddenly frowned.

"I have no idea." I shrugged. "Should I call and ask her?"

"No, no." She pursed her lips. "I'm sure she would have said if she was."

"Who is she?" Zane interrupted us with a confused look. "Who are you two talking about?"

"Robin." Lucky and I said at the same time and laughed.

"And Robin is who?" Zane looked just as confused, and I caught him glaring at the intersection of my arm with Lucky's.

"The girl from the restaurant last week." Lucky detached herself from me and walked over and gave him a big kiss and put her arms around his neck. "I would have thought you would have remembered her, the way you were going on about her."

"The restaurant?" He kissed her back and ran his hands up and down her back. "Oh, the bitch?" He looked at me in surprise. "I know I joked around and told you she wanted you, but I was just joking, bro, no need to follow up on it."

"I totally asked her out because you told me she wanted me." I rolled my eyes at him and then looked at Lucky. "How did he get you? You seem like too smart a girl to fall for my dumbass brother."

"Watch your mouth." Zane grinned at me. "She recognized an awesome guy when she saw one."

"I did?" Lucky blinked. "Where is he?"

"See what you've done now, Noah?" He tickled Lucky and she squealed as she tried to get away from him.

"Stop," she cried out as she laughed. "I need to help Noah."

"See what you have to look forward to?" Zane pulled Lucky towards him and held her in his arms and kissed her head.

"Doesn't look so bad."

"It's not so bad. She's not so bad. I think I'll keep her."

"Really, Zane Beaumont?" She glared up at him.

"Uh oh. I better leave you guys to it, before she decides to call off the wedding." Zane made a face and I laughed.

"Have you guys set a date yet?"

"No." Lucky shook her head. "I can't decide if we should get married before or after the babies are born."

"I say we fly to Vegas tomorrow and just get it over with." Zane grinned. "We could have Elvis serenade us."

"Yeah, why not?" Lucky rolled her eyes. "Idiot." She mumbled under her breath and winked at me. "Now let's talk dinner. How's about steak, herb-roasted potatoes and a big salad?"

"If I get to make the salad," I laughed. "Or grill the steak. I have no idea how to make herb-roasted potatoes."

"So do you like Robin?" Lucky looked at me quizzically. "Like a lot?"

"Lucky, he just met the girl. Give him a chance to get to know her before you have us at a double wedding."

"I do think I like her." I nodded slowly. "At least, what I know of her so far seems pretty great."

"So this may be the first of many dates?" Lucky looked excited. "Like we could go on a double date sometime soon?"

"Slow down, there." I laughed, and watched as Zane gave me a look as if to say 'I told you so.' "Let's get through this dinner first."

"She's very beautiful." Lucky stared at me. "I mean, she was a bit of a shrew, but she's beautiful."

"She apologized to me." I saw them look at me in surprise. "I saw her the other day when I was running. She's nice, nicer than that day in the restaurant."

"It's the waitresses these days. They think they can talk to you any way that they want." Zane laughed as Lucky hit him in the arm. "But I wouldn't have it any other way."

"Ass." Lucky shook her head at him. "But I'm glad you like her. I think she seemed pretty nice."

"Yeah. I think I'm willing to give it a chance. See where it goes." I was surprised at the words as they came out of my mouth. I hadn't realized until that moment that I really was interested in seeing how everything went. "I think it's time for me to move on with my life." I smiled at them both briefly. "Now, shall we get cooking?"

"Yes, Zane go and get the ..." Lucky started talking, but I was distracted by my ringing phone.

"Excuse me." I pulled my phone out of my pocket. "I hope that's not Robin calling to cancel already." I joked and then looked at the screen. All the blood drained out of my face as I saw the name flashing on my phone. It was Skylar. My heart stopped for a moment as I stared at the phone. Questions ran through my brain as I hurried out of the kitchen to answer the call.

"Hello." I whispered into the phone, all thoughts of Robin dropping out of my mind. "Skylar, is that you?"

CHAPTER SEVEN

"SKYLAR," I SAID AGAIN, BUT THEN I heard a click and there was dead silence on the other side. I immediately tried to call the number back again, but it just rang and rang without going to voicemail. "Damn it," I cursed under my breath. My stomach was in knots and I wasn't sure how I was going to continue on with the night. It was like life didn't want me to move on just yet. Maybe it hadn't been a good idea to invite Robin over for dinner. It had been an impetuous invitation and now I was regretting it. I tried calling the number again and nearly threw my phone across the room when she didn't answer. I was worried. I knew that she wouldn't call me unless it was important. Unless it was a set-up. I closed my eyes and leaned against the wall, not knowing what to do. Part of me thought I should just catch a plane to Orlando and then drive to Palm Bonita and do whatever I could to get to Skylar.

"Noah," Zane walked out of the kitchen and stared at me with a look of worry on his face. "You okay? Who was that?"

"I'm fine." I gave him a weak smile and started to walk away from him.

"Was it Mom?" His voice sounded angry, and I shook my head as I continued walking. "Was it Mom?" His voice was louder as he followed behind me.

"No." I turned around and looked him in the eyes. "No, it wasn't."

"She has your number, though?"

"Yes." I couldn't lie to him, even though I wanted to.

"And she calls you?" His eyes looked bleak and I didn't want to have this conversation now, but I was angry and annoyed.

"Yes, she calls me. But I'm not talking to her anymore."

"Well, I'm glad you have that option." He looked angry and confused. "You're going to have to forgive me if I'm being a jackass here, but what the fuck is going on? I really don't understand it. Our mother won't say jack shit to me even when I fly halfway across the world to see her. Yet she's calling you every fucking Friday and telling you how much she loves you?"

"That wasn't her." I shook my head. "And she doesn't call me often. She hasn't called me in a while. I haven't seen or spoken to her in over a year."

"Why not? You're the brother who always wanted to find her. Why haven't you set up a big family reunion already to show me that you were right all along and dear old Mummy was back?"

"Maybe I was wrong. Maybe it was best for us not to find her." I stared into his eyes, willing him to see and understand where I was coming from. "She doesn't know the meaning of right and wrong, Zane. She doesn't know what true love is. We were better off without her. We still have each other."

"Well, she clearly wants you and her new son. What am I? Pig fat?" He walked towards the front door. "I can't do this right now. I'm going out."

"Wait." I touched his shoulder. "Don't be like that."

"Why not?" He glared at me and brushed my hand off of him. "You're clearly not in a talking mood."

"I'm sorry." I took a big breath. "And I'm really confused right now. I could really use your support right now."

"What's wrong?" He froze and looked at me with a worried expression. "Are you sick, Noah?"

I shook my head, unable to speak, as he stared at me with extreme love and concern. My heart swelled for the man who was my brother and best friend. The man who looked out for me even when he was hurt inside. The man I knew would do anything for me; actually, had done everything for me. And I knew that I couldn't take the easy way out. I knew that the easy way out might make it better for me, but it would break his heart and I couldn't do that.

"Are you gay?" He continued. "Is that why you're confused? You know I will love you no matter what, right? I told Lucky not to push you into getting a girlfriend. I'm so sorry, bro, I never meant for you to—"

"Zane, I'm not gay." I laughed and shook my head in amusement. "Though, I do appreciate your support if I was."

"I was about to say, my gaydar is totally off." He laughed along with me, and for a few moments we had an easy camaraderie.

"I met someone in Palm Bonita. I told you that already." I paused. "But it's a lot more complicated than I told you about."

"Oh, shit." Zane's eyes widened. "Did you get her pregnant?"

"No." I rolled my eyes. "And to be fair, that's a bit of a funny question coming from you."

"Huh?" He looked at me blankly and then laughed. "Well, you know. I'm the older brother. It's okay if I make mistakes."

"I heard that, Zane." Lucky's voice called out from behind us. "It's nice to know our babies are your mistake."

"I didn't mean that." Zane made a face at me and then looked at Lucky with pleading eyes. "You know I love you and our babies." He continued and Lucky groaned, and smiled at me.

"Uh huh."

"That was just a foot-in-mouth moment."

"You mean it was a that-shouldn't-have-been-heard-by-the-fiancée moment!" She walked over to him and socked him in the shoulder. "You're lucky that I'm not going to get mad at that comment."

"You're not?" He grinned at her happily.

"No," She smiled at me. "But only because Noah is trying to tell you something and you haven't given him the opportunity to get it out."

"But you're the one that keeps talking." He frowned at her. "Not me."

"You're talking right now."

"But you're talking right now as well."

"But you just continued talking, even though you know Noah is waiting."

"So did you." He stuck his tongue out at her and she leaned in to kiss him. "Don't start something you can't continue." He whispered as his arms circled her and I groaned at them.

"You two need to get a room." I shook my head and Lucky disentangled herself from Zane and walked over to me.

"Not right now, we don't. You guys need to go and talk about whatever's bothering you." She pushed me towards Zane. "Go in the living room. I'll get dinner ready."

"But what about the salad?"

"You'll make it next time." She smiled at me gently. "And trust me, I'll hold you to that."

"Are you sure?"

"I'm sure." She smiled again before walking back towards the kitchen and my heart filled with even more love for her. It was weird that I had only known her for a few weeks, because she already felt like my family.

"Wait." I called out to her and she turned around with a surprised look.

"Yes?"

"I want you to come in the living room as well. I want to tell you both what I have to say." I looked at them back and forth and felt waves of happiness and jealousy wash over me as I saw Lucky and Zane exchange a look of love and bliss.

"Really? Are you sure? You don't have to tell me."

"You're my family now, Lucky. I want you to know. Plus, I'm sure Zane would tell you anyways."

"No, he would never break your confidence," Lucky protested, but I held up my hand to stop her.

"I don't mind if he does. Not with you. You're the woman he loves, the mother of his unborn children, shoot, you're the mother of my niece and nephew. I want him to tell you. You shouldn't have secrets. Not with the one you love. Not with your life partner."

"You sound like you're talking from experience, bro," Zane questioned me and I sighed as I walked to the living room with them and we all sat down. I took a deep breath before beginning. I held up my phone and started, "The phone call I got just now was from a girl named Skylar. She's a girl that I met in Palm Bonita. She's the girl I can't stop thinking about. The girl who makes me wish I could move mountains." I paused and gave them a rueful smile. "She's the girl who made me realize that love and family isn't based on bloodlines and that it isn't always pretty. She's also the girl who hates me with all her heart." I looked at the floor then and took a deep breath. My heart was beating so quickly that I thought that I was going to have a heart attack. I felt like I couldn't breathe and that the pain in my chest might end my life before I had a chance to do anything meaningful.

"What happened in Palm Bonita, Noah?" Zane's expression was as soft as his tone and I wondered at how he was able to go from angry to caring in mere minutes.

"When I arrived in Palm Bonita, I met a girl. She was exciting and carefree and we got into a relationship pretty quickly." I sighed. "It wasn't something I had planned or wanted, but I was angry at the situation I was in, and I was missing you and my life. I needed something to take the time and pain away. She offered me solace, in and out of the bed. And I jumped at the chance to get away, mentally and physically, from everything that was going on." I paused to make sure that I wasn't going too fast. "But she wasn't who I thought she was."

"She wasn't?" Lucky prodded after a long silence.

"No." I shook my head.

"How so?" Lucky's eyes were wide.

"For one, she was married." I saw Lucky's mouth drop open and Zane gave me an amused look. "She wasn't living with the husband or anything. She was actually in Palm Bonita because she wanted to get away from him."

"That's not so bad, then." Lucky gave me an encouraging look. "If you thought she was going to get divorced."

"I didn't even know she was married until the end." I shrugged. "Though all the signs were there."

"Is that why you broke up?" Lucky asked again and then bit her lip. "Sorry, I didn't mean to imply that …"

"You don't have to be sorry for anything." I gave her a reassuring smile. "But no, that's not why we broke up. I realized she wasn't the person I thought she was."

"Because she lied to you about being married?"

"No. You would think that would be it, right?" I chortled to myself, not believing that I was actually talking about everything.

"So what was it?" Zane's voice was impatient and I held back a laugh. Trust my brother to want to get to the meaty part of the story right away.

"There was this girl, another girl in town. Well, she and I became friendly. More than friendly, and I developed feelings for her." I paused, not sure how to continue with the story. "Well, the girl I was dating didn't like that. And she treated the new girl badly." I knew that I was being vague, but for some reason I didn't want to tell them everything about our relationship. It was too close to home and too painful.

"So you cheated on your girlfriend?" Lucky looked at me in disappointment.

"He can't cheat if she's married." Zane gave her a look and I felt a surge of love toward him for sticking up for me.

"I didn't cheat." I said emphatically. "In fact, we continued dating. I thought I could convince her to treat the other girl better. But it backfired. And I found out that I had ruined everything." I closed my eyes as I thought about the bleakness in Skylar's eyes as she realized that I wasn't going to be her savior. That no matter how much I wanted to be the one to save her from her life, I couldn't. I think both of our hearts broke that day. And there was nothing either one of us could do to change the facts. It was harder for her to accept because she still had faith and believed in miracles. But I knew that there wasn't going to be a miracle; there would be no parting of the Red Sea. I was no Moses.

"Are you okay, Noah?" Lucky's voice sounded worried, and I opened my eyes slowly. I stared at the two of them on the couch, snuggled into each other's arms, and I envied them. I envied how perfect their life was and how lucky they were to have found each other. How simple everything had been for them. It was what I thought my life was going to be like.

"I can still remember the day that I realized I loved Skylar." I talked without making eye contact with either of them. "We'd gone to the park and she wanted to go to the swings, and of course she wanted me to actually swing as well. I'd laughed, of course, because there were a bunch of little kids and I felt like a creep taking over one of the swings, but the joy on her face dissipated any feelings of worry or concern. Of course, I only stayed on the swing for a few minutes since I still felt slightly self-conscious. A grown man swinging on a swing in the middle of the day is not cute."

"It sounds pretty adorable to me." Lucky grinned and I smiled back at her before I continued talking.

"So, I decided to push her, so that she could go higher and higher. And she started laughing in delight. And she let go of the handles and put her hands in the air and she squealed out that she felt like she was flying. And I laughed and told her that I wished that I could fly.

And she looked back at me and said, 'Every time I'm with you, I feel like I'm flying.'"

I stopped talking as my throat grew dry. I could still picture the open joy and honesty in her eyes as she grinned at me, a purely happy smile full of love and trust. "And I told her that every time I was with her, I felt like I could fly." I stopped talking as emotions overtook me. "It was a perfect moment and I realized that love can hit you in the most unexpected ways."

"If you still love Skylar, maybe you can try and date her still." Lucky sounded hopeful.

"What?" I looked at her in confusion. "I don't think you understand. Skylar is—"

"Don't push him, Lucky." Zane interrupted me. "He obviously wants to move on from what went down in Palm Bonita. I'm not trying to be rude, but it seems to me like that relationship was a rollercoaster ride and a bumpy one at that."

"But true love only comes around once in a lifetime." Lucky glared at him and shifted away from him in her seat.

"Says who?" Zane shook his head. "He's obviously trying to move on. Maybe you should—"

"I'm still here, guys." I cleared my throat, not wanting to talk about it anymore. I didn't have the energy to explain to them that they had misunderstood what I was saying. "But, yeah, the point of telling you guys all that is to explain why I'm still a bit emotional about everything. Especially getting Skylar's call."

"Do you still want to have the dinner tonight? With Robin?" Lucky jumped up and walked over to me. "You can cancel and blame it on me if you want."

"No." I jumped up. "I still want her to come over. You guys are right. I need to move on. I need to refocus."

"Yeah, please do. I want some answers sometime this year." Zane stared at me as he walked over to Lucky and rubbed her shoulder. She glared at him and he gave her an apologetic smile; within a few seconds they were holding hands.

"Give it a rest, Zane." Lucky sighed.

"I'm trying." He sighed as well, and I looked over at them both with a rueful smile.

"You guys are lucky to have each other. Always remember that."

"You hear that, Lucky?" Zane grinned at her and pulled her into his arms. "You're lucky to have me." He kissed her forehead as she rolled her eyes at him. "But really I'm the fortunate one. I'm the real winner. I found you, somehow tricked you into falling in love with me, and now you're stuck with me forever."

"Oh, boy." She shuddered and laughed as he smacked her bottom.

"You're my forever love and I'm never letting go of you."

"Not even when I shower?" She grinned at him and wiggled her eyebrows and he slid his hand up her back.

"Especially not when you shower." He grinned at her before leaning down to kiss her on the lips. I stood there watching them, still slightly shocked to see my previously cold and emotionless brother acting like some sort of Romeo.

"Sorry, Noah." Lucky pulled away from Zane's embrace with a flush. "Zane just gets carried away."

"I guess I know how the babies happened." I laughed and she blushed even redder.

"Noah!" Zane winked at me, as he faked a disapproving voice.

"Sorry." I winked back at him and stretched. "I'm going to leave you two lovebirds alone and go upstairs." I left the room and tried to ignore the empty pit of despair in my stomach. I brightened up at the thought of Robin joining us for dinner. A part of me was buzzing with excitement as I thought about getting to know her better. But then I thought of Skylar and her phone call and all excitement left me. Instead I was filled with guilt and concern and I wasn't sure if those feelings would ever leave me.

***

"Dinner was wonderful. Thank you, Lucky." Robin licked her lips, and we all laughed at her obvious enjoyment of the food. "I haven't had a good meal in a long while."

"Well, you know, us waitresses have to stick together." Lucky laughed and stood up. "Now for dessert. Zane, help me with the dishes, please."

"Huh?" He looked up at her and she gave him a look before he jumped up as well. "Oh, sure." He looked over at me and made a face. "It seems like my daily chores have already started."

"Zane Beaumont, helping me clear the table once doesn't count as daily chores." Lucky's voice was amused and exasperated at the same time.

"Well, you already had me do a grocery run."

"Zane, you went to get yourself some beer and I asked you to grab some ice cream. That is not a grocery run."

"It sounds like she has you beat, Zane." Robin laughed as she watched them banter and she turned to me, her eyes sparkling. "Is it like this every day?"

"Yup." I grinned back at her. "I feel like I'm part man, part judge. Well, maybe not judge. More like mediator."

"And here I thought you were the big bad wolf." Robin leaned towards me flirtatiously.

"I can be if you want me to be." I leaned towards her.

"Oh, shit, please tell me I do not sound like such an idiot." Zane shuddered and Lucky pushed him towards the kitchen with an apologetic look.

"They're really cute." Robin smiled as they left the room.

"Yeah." I agreed. "They're perfect for each other."

"It must be nice to live with such an obviously in love couple." She tilted her head and stared into my eyes. "A real life example that true love can and does exist."

"When it's not annoying as hell." I made a face. "Seriously though, I couldn't be happier for my brother. He found a gem."

"I can't believe she was a waitress."

"I guess there is something about the men in my family being attracted to the help." I wiggled my eyebrows at her and then groaned as I realized what I had said. "Oh, my God, I so didn't mean that as it came out."

"It's okay." She laughed at my look of terror. "I'm not going to bite your head off. *This* time."

"I'm glad to hear that." I ran my hands through my hair and sat back. "I seem to have a knack of putting my foot in my mouth."

"Well, you do have a very nice mouth." She stared at my lips and I wanted to grab her and pull her towards me and kiss her hard. I had been captivated by Robin as soon as she had stepped through the door in her slinky black dress. She was terribly overdressed for dinner but she looked sexy as hell. It didn't hurt that she also smelled divine. The way she ate was also titillating and I wondered if she was trying to seduce me. My loins felt heavy and hard and I groaned at how typically male I was. All I could think about was getting her into my bed. And the last time I had followed the needs of my body, I had been burned badly.

"I've heard that one before," I mumbled, not thinking, and she laughed.

"Modest, aren't you, Noah?"

"Dang it. I'm an idiot." I jumped up and pulled her up with me. "Sorry, I'm distracted by your beauty. Let me make it up to you."

"How would you like to make it up to me?" She raised an eyebrow. "And please don't tell me in the bedroom or I will walk right out the door."

"Well, there goes that plan." I pulled her towards me and looked down into her eyes with a naughty look. My arms circled her waist and I brought her body into mine so that she could feel just how turned on I was. "But I suppose I'll allow you to disappoint me."

"Your body is hard." She gulped as she stared up at her. Her hands were on my arms and I flexed my muscles for her. "I mean your arms are hard. Your muscles, you know. Nothing else. Is hard. You know what I mean." Her face flushed and she stopped talking for a moment. "Shit, I think you've rubbed off on me."

"Really?" I held back a laugh. "I'm hard and I've rubbed off on you?" I moved my head closer to hers and whispered against her lips. "Don't you think that's a bit much for a first date?"

Robin's face was bright red, and she attempted to move away from me in embarrassment. I kept her firmly pressed against me and then leaned down and kissed her. As my lips touched her, I felt a jolt of electricity pass through us and her eyes widened in shock as I slipped my tongue roughly into her mouth and cupped her ass to bring her in even closer to me. I laughed as I felt her teeth nibble on my lower lip, and then I groaned as her fingers reached into the back of my shirt and she ran her fingernails up and down my back. Robin pressed her breasts against my chest and all I wanted to do was rip her shirt off and then throw her bra across the room before I sucked on her nipples. I felt feverish as we kissed and I felt suddenly bereft when she pulled away from me with a reluctant look.

"Sorry." She looked away from me. "Like I said before, I'm not on the menu for tonight. If that disappoints you, I can just leave." Her tone became slightly edgy and I felt the mood between us change.

"Hey," I grabbed her chin and made her look at me. "You're jumping to conclusions again."

"Excuse me?" She glared at me and pulled away and I wondered how women were able to change their moods so quickly.

"You're acting like you did in the restaurant. You're judging me and my actions and basing your words on emotions that are running though you. Those emotions are not because of what I've said or done. I've given you no reason to think that all I want from you is sex."

"I never said that is all you want." She sputtered, her eyelashes blinking rapidly. "I never said that at all."

"That's what you thought and implied when you said you were just going to leave." I grabbed a hold of her hands and drew her into me again. This time I didn't bring her close enough to feel the hardness in my pants. "I'm not going to lie and say I'm not attracted to you. I'm not going to tell you that I don't want to make love to you. I wouldn't be a normal heterosexual man if I didn't. But that's not all that I want from you. And it wasn't what I was implying. When I stood up from the table, I was going to ask you if you wanted to dance. And not a lap dance or a striptease. Just a regular dance with two normal people who are on a first date and getting to know each other."

"You want to *dance*?" Robin made a face. "I did hear that correctly, right? You said you want to dance?"

"Yes." I nodded and smiled. I pulled away from her, counted to three in my head and proceeded to waltz around the room by myself. Robin watched me with amazement in her eyes as I glided around the dining room, and I continued on with my movements, pretending to dip and twirl my invisible partner before finding my way back in front of her and dipping in a slow and low bow. As I straightened up, Robin's eyes watched me mirthfully and she clapped enthusiastically, grinning at me as I pretended to preen at her adoration and praise.

"Encore, encore." She laughed and I shook my head.

"Not unless I have a partner."

"I'm not really a good ballroom dancer." She made a face. "I'm more a getting low type of girl."

"Getting low?"

"You know, to hip hop." She laughed and did a dance move where she shook her hips as she moved down to the floor. I watched, mesmerized, as she moved her body rhythmically, and all I could think about was her moving that way on top of me. She stood up straight and looked at me quizzically as I just stood there staring at her, unspeaking.

I didn't know what to say. I wanted her. I felt a connection with her that I'd never felt before but I had nothing to offer her. I was still in limbo; everything in my life was in flux. I wasn't good enough for her. It wouldn't be fair to her to try and start a relationship. It didn't matter that my heart sung when she smiled at me with that happy but uncertain look in her eyes. It didn't matter that I heard birds sing when she said my name. It didn't matter that when I was with her I started to feel alive again.

"You do know what hip-hop is, right?" she asked uncertainly and I nodded, still unable to talk. I was transfixed by her beauty and the fragile air around her. Robin put on a good confident show, but I could tell that there was a lot more to her than the exterior she was showing me. Something told me that inside, she was made of glass and that she would shatter if I made one wrong move.

"Yes, yes. I know." I finally spoke and took a step back. "I've jumped on it a few times." I winked at her and she laughed as she got my little joke.

"Thanks for inviting me to dinner." She looked away from me, and I knew she could sense the sudden awkwardness between us. I didn't know what to say to her. Five minutes ago we were making out then we were arguing and then we were laughing and now we were in that awkward space that comes between two people who aren't sure of what the other person is thinking.

"I'm so glad that you could make it." I nodded, all thoughts of dancing gone from my mind. "Would you like to stay for dessert?"

"I should be going!" She shook her head and I saw a glimpse of an emotion close to fear in her eyes. "I have to practice my monologue for an audition," she explained. "But it's been really wonderful."

"We should do it again." I smiled at her, but our eyes didn't connect. We had lost that special moment and now we were acting like two people who barely knew each other and didn't want to get closer.

"Yes. Definitely. Please let Zane and Lucky know that I had a great time and thank them for the wonderful dinner."

"Thank you for bringing the wine." I nodded and walked with her to the front door. Part of me was prodding myself to say something, to not let the evening end like this. It had been a good night. We had a connection. I knew she had to feel it as well. I wondered what was holding her back. What was her story? I wanted to know everything about her. I wanted her to regain her trust in men. Let her know that she didn't have to be on the defensive all the time. We weren't all bad. I wanted to hold her close to me and let her warmth sink into me so that I no longer felt cold and lonely. Instead I opened the front door and gave her a big smile. "Good luck with the audition."

"Thanks." She nodded and fiddled with her car keys as she walked out the door.

"I'll call you," I lied as she smiled at me weakly and hurried away. I closed the door slowly and fell back, not sure what had happened to our easy rapport. It was as if both of us had sensed that we had chemistry but neither one of us was interested in moving forward with it. But it was more than that: it was as if both of us were interested but we were too scared to do anything about it.

"Hey, where's Robin?" Lucky walked out from the dining area and looked around.

"She left."

"She left?" Lucky frowned. "I just put the apple pie on the table. I even made homemade ice-cream with the Kitchen-Aid that Zane got me."

"Sorry, she had to leave." I walked towards her and took her arm in mine. "But I can eat her helping and mine if you want."

"I don't understand why she left." Lucky looked at me with narrow eyes. "You guys were getting on so well. What happened?"

"I think we both realized that perhaps it's best for us to not go down this road."

"What road?" Lucky's voice rose and she sounded annoyed. "This was barely a first date. No one's asking you guys to get married. Get to know each other. Eat some pie."

"It's not that simple." I rubbed my eyes, suddenly feeling very tired. "I think we both felt a connection and I think it scared us both. I'm not in any position to start a new relationship, Lucky. I don't want to hurt her."

"Why aren't you in a position?" She sighed. "Do you want to get back with the girl you dated in Palm Bonita?"

"No."

"Then what? You're back here now, Noah. You're not in Palm Bonita anymore. You have to move on with your life. You can't live in the past. This is now. This is new. This is called moving forward. Nothing good happens if you stay stagnant." She grabbed ahold of my shoulders and looked deeply into my eyes. "Trust me, you have to make a decision, Noah. You can let the past haunt you. You can keep all the secrets you want, but eventually it's going to catch up with you. Eventually it's going to be too much. Don't let that happen. You need to live for you now. You need to live for the *now*. Stop holding in the hurt and pushing people away. One day you're going to wake up and there's going to be no one waiting anymore."

She kissed me on the cheek and then walked away from me. I stood there contemplating her words. She was right. I needed to move on. But I knew I couldn't move on without making everything right. I needed to try one more time to get Skylar. My conscience wouldn't forgive me if I didn't.

CHAPTER EIGHT

"ZANE, DO YOU THINK THAT RIGHT *now, at this very moment, Mom is staring at the stars as well and thinking about us?" I looked over at my brother as we lay on our backs and stared up at the sky.*

"No."

"I think she is. I think she's most probably waiting for a shooting star so that she can make a wish. And she's wishing that she can find us and come back to us and smother us with hugs and kisses." I spoke wistfully and tried to ignore the tears that were creeping into the corners of my eyes. At ten years old, I still hadn't

perfected the art of not crying when I felt sad. Not like Zane had. He never showed any emotion.

"Then you're an imbecile." Zane turned towards me with a frown.

"What's an im-be-ceil?" I asked him, not understanding what he meant.

"Nothing, Noah. Just be quiet."

"I'm glad Dad let us go camping this weekend," I continued excitedly.

"Dad didn't let us do anything." Zane sighed. "And we aren't camping, idiot. We're lying on bedsheets in the back garden. We don't have tents or sleeping bags. We don't have a bonfire. We don't have anyone telling us scary stories. It's just us lying here on a dirty bedsheet, looking up at some stars that we can barely see because of all the pollution."

"It's still fun, though." I reached over and squeezed his hand. "I'm glad that it's just us. We're like two warriors staring up at the night sky waiting for the sun to rise and take us on our next journey."

"Yeah." He sighed but smiled at me. "We're two warriors."

"I'm Conan." I growled into the air and shouted. "I'm Conan, so nobody better mess with me or my brother Zane."

"Shhhhh." Zane placed his dirty hand over my mouth. "Be quiet. If Dad hears us out here, we'll be in trouble."

"I thought you said he said it was okay?" I looked at him in confusion and yawned.

"Just go to sleep, Noah, you're tired." Zane shook his head and lay back, looking up at the stars. I was quiet for a moment, but I still wasn't tired enough to go to sleep.

"We'll always be brothers, right, Zane?" I spoke lightly, scared that I was going to upset him again.

"What are you talking about?" He rolled over and looked at me with his older brother frown.

"You won't leave me, right?" I bit my lower lip and opened my eyes wide so no tears fell. I wanted to be a big boy. I didn't want Zane to make fun of me and call me a baby. "You won't go away like Mom?"

He didn't say anything for a moment as he lay there staring at me. Then he reached over and hugged me and whispered in my ear. "I'm your big brother. You're never going to get rid of me."

"Never?" I asked hopefully.

"Never." He let me go and stared at me. "We're birds of a feather, Noah. We could be the same person. We have exactly the same blood running through our veins. We're family. We are all we got. I will never leave you. You're stuck with me."

"Just don't try and eat all my candy." I lay back and grinned, everything all right in my world again. "We may be brothers and we may have the same blood, but all my candy is still mine."

"I'll think about it." He laughed and lay back at the sky before pointing up to something quickly. "Look, Noah. There's a shooting star. There's a shooting star. Quick, make a wish."

We both closed our eyes and mumbled our wishes. I wished that I would never have to go a day without Zane by my side. And then opened my eyes. "What did you wish for, Zane?"

"I can't say." He mumbled and his voice sounded hoarse.

"Tell me." I pleaded. "Please."

"I can't tell you, Noah. If I tell you, it won't come true."

I spent the next week making plans for the documentary and trying to call Skylar back. Unfortunately, her phone number was now disconnected and I had no other way to get in contact with her. Well, I had one way, but I knew that nothing good could come from going that route. So I threw myself into my work and tried to avoid Zane and Lucky as much as possible. I didn't want to deal with their questions or concern. I knew that they meant well and I knew that Zane just wanted some answers, but I still wasn't sure how I was going to deal with everything. I also hadn't spoken to Robin either, even though I had been thinking about her every day since the dinner. I wanted to call her so badly, but I didn't know what to say. "Hey, I think I like you. I know I want to kiss you and make love to you. But I'm kind of fucked up in the head right now, and I'm scared that I'm going to hurt you and you're going to break like shattered glass."

So I didn't call, but every night I saw her face haunting me in my dreams. However, I didn't dread going to bed anymore. Not when I knew that I would have visions of her and her green-brown eyes sparkling at and teasing me. I had finally decided to give her a call when I got a call from an unknown number. Skylar immediately popped to mind and I answered the phone eagerly.

"Hello," I gasped, scared that the other person was going to click off.

"Noah, *mon cheri?*"

"Mom?" I walked to my bedroom door and closed it before going back to sit on my bed.

"Noah." Her voice sounded emotional. "You haven't called me."

"I haven't had anything to say."

"I heard you're back in Los Angeles."

"How did you know that?"

"Your father." Her voice was light and pained.

"You spoke to him." I frowned. I had no idea that she had been in contact with my dad.

"*Oui*, I mean yes." She sighed. "His last two checks have been late. I had to call him to make sure that he wasn't going to stop providing me with my means to live."

"You mean the hush money?" I said coldly into the phone.

"It's not like that, Noah. I need this money. It's how we live."

"What do you want?" I said impatiently, not wanting to talk to her.

"Your father says he hasn't heard from you since you've been back."

"He hasn't rushed to see me." I laughed bitterly. "You'd think he'd want to see his dead son back from the grave."

"Noah, that's not fair."

"You're sticking up from him?" I said disbelievingly. "I thought you hated him."

"I do hate him." She sighed. "But he is still your father."

"He's my father only by way of my genes." I scoffed. "He's not my family. He doesn't care about me."

"But I care about you, Noah. I want to see you. Will you come visit your mama in Paris?"

"Do you want me to come alone, or to bring Zane and his fiancée Lucky with me?"

"I don't even know who this Lucky person is." Her voice sounded annoyed and vacant. "Why would I want to see her? I want to see my son."

"You met Lucky when she went to Paris with Zane." My voice was hard. "And yes, I know that you pretended you didn't know who he was. How could you do that?"

"It was for your safety, my dear boy. I didn't want to accidentally slip and tell them you were still alive. You told me that it was imperative that I told no one. Absolutely no one, you said. I was just doing as you said."

"I didn't tell you to pretend that you didn't recognize your own son." I shouted, angry that she could be so obtuse. "What sort of mother are you?"

"He is not my son, Noah." Her voice was angry. "You are my son. You are my love. You are the one I have missed every day. You are my blood."

"You raised Zane as well." I shouted wanting to punch something hard. "He thinks you are his mother. He has happy memories of you."

"It is a lie!" she cried. "I will not live a lie anymore. It was all too much. My life was a lie. I couldn't take it. I won't live a lie anymore."

"You told him to look after me. You told him to be a good big brother and protect me." I spoke words that I didn't even know I was thinking. "It just doesn't make sense."

"He always looked after you." She sighed. "I knew from the day that you were born that he would protect you with his life. You were safer with him than with me. I had postpartum depression, I couldn't think straight. I was scared that I would hurt you. And I would never have been able to live with myself if I had hurt you, my precious son."

"So you trusted and loved him enough to have him look after me when you walked away. He was a little kid, Mom. He didn't do anything to you."

"He was too much like your father." Her voice quivered. "He looked just like your father. It was too much for me. Every time I looked at him, I felt a mixture of emotions. I wanted to love him. In my way, I tried to love him. I just couldn't love him as I love you, my son.

Please come to Paris and visit me. I miss you. I want to see you. Forgive me, Noah. Forgive me for leaving you. Forgive me for being a poor mother. Please understand that I've never stopped loving you. You have always been in my heart, just like the blood that pumps through my veins."

"Zane is my family. It's my turn to protect him now." My voice was cold as I spoke into the phone. "I will not come to visit you. I will not have his heart broken."

"Tell him, Noah," she cried out. "You need to tell him the truth."

"No." I shook my head vehemently. "It would kill him."

"He deserves to know the truth. You cannot hide it from him. It is not fair of you to play God."

"It wasn't fair when you walked out and left us brokenhearted. I won't have him go through that again."

"It is not my fault. I beg of you, Noah. Please come and see me."

"If you cannot love my brother as your own, then you cannot love me." I spoke slowly. "Goodbye,

Mother." I hung up the phone and powered it off, and sat on the bed just staring into space. A few minutes later, I heard a knock at the door and ignored it.

"Noah?" Lucky opened the door slowly, and poked her head around the door. She stood there hesitating. "Can I come in?"

"Not now." I looked away from her, willing her to go away. I didn't want to talk to anyone at that moment.

"We have to go the Johnsons' now." She stepped into the room. "They're expecting us."

"Shit, I forgot that was today." I sighed and jumped up, still avoiding her gaze. "Okay, let's go."

"Noah, wait." She bit her lip and walked over to me. She had tears in her eyes and as I studied her face, I could see that she looked distraught.

"Oh, my God, Lucky. What's wrong?" I studied her face anxiously, worry for her consuming me. "Is it the babies?"

"No." She sobbed and tears streamed from her eyes. "It's not the babies."

"What's wrong, Lucky? Oh, my God, is it Zane? What happened to my brother?"

"It's not Zane." She started crying even more and I stared at her hopelessly.

"What is it, Lucky? What's wrong? Oh, dear God, you're not leaving my brother, are you?" Dread and fear filled me at the possibility. If Lucky left Zane, he would be devastated for the rest of his life. I knew that there was no way that he would ever get over losing Lucky.

"No." She gave me a small smile. "Of course I'm not leaving him. I love him."

"Lucky, you're killing me here. What's wrong?" I shook my head in exasperation. "Why are you crying?"

"I didn't mean to listen." She sobbed out. "I came to knock on your door to tell you that it was time to leave, but I heard you shouting, so I decided to wait until you got off the phone and I heard what you said."

"What?" I froze still.

"I heard what you said, Noah." Her eyes looked at me wildly and sorrowfully.

"I don't know what you mean." I shook my head and looked away from her.

"It's true, isn't it?" She sat on my bed and wiped her eyes on her sleeve. "I guess it makes sense. I mean, not really, but it adds up."

"I don't know what …" I paused as she looked at me with her big brown eyes full of love and concern for me. "Okay, it's true." I sighed. "Zane and I don't have the same mom."

CHAPTER NINE

"YOU HAVE TO TELL HIM," LUCKY'S tears dried up on the car ride over to the Johnsons'. "You can't keep this inside. It's not healthy for you and it's not good for Zane, either. He needs to know the truth."

"I don't want to break his heart." I shook my head. "You have to keep this a secret."

"Noah." She sighed. "I don't know if I can keep this from him."

"Let me do this in my own way." I looked at her, with my eyes begging her for a reprieve. "Please."

"He's going to be at the Johnsons'." She took a deep breath. "We have a surprise for you. I'm sorry."

"Oh, no." I looked at her in fear. "What did you do?"

"I'm sorry, Noah, but Zane went and picked Robin up. She will most probably be inside with the Johnsons as well."

"What?" I shouted. "Why would you do that?"

"You've been so lonely this last week. I know you guys had an attraction and I convinced Zane that it was in your best interest to bring her over this afternoon. I'm sorry."

"Fuck, I can't believe you did that." I clenched my fists. "I don't need you interfering with my love life, Lucky."

"I'm sorry." She looked at me with huge eyes. "I made a mistake. I thought it would help. I didn't realize, well, you know. I didn't realize that you had so much going on."

"I have nothing to say to Robin, Lucky. If I wanted to talk to her, I would have called her and asked her out on a date."

"I don't believe you." She shook her head. "You're scared, Noah. I don't know what that girl did to you in Palm Bonita, but you don't owe her anything. She missed out. You're a good guy and you deserve better."

"I don't *miss* the girl I dated." I sighed. "You have it all wrong. It's a lot more complicated than you think."

"Well, maybe if you didn't keep everything to yourself I'd know why you're still so hung up on Skylar, who frankly sounds like a bit of a bitch."

"You have no idea what you're talking about, Lucky." I shook my head and got out of the car. "You have absolutely no idea."

"I'm sorry, Noah. I'm just trying to help."

"You don't understand, Lucky. You can't help me. I'm not Zane, you can't save me." I shook my head and then lowered my voice as I saw the hurt expression on her face. "Look, I know you're trying to help. But this is not something you can fix." I grabbed her hand. "Maybe in another life, in another world." I shrugged as

I stared into her face. "Like I said before, Zane won the jackpot when he found you, Lucky. If he hadn't found you first, I would have done my darndest to get you for myself." I laughed at the shocked look on her face. "Don't worry, I'm not trying to steal you away. I just want you to know that I appreciate you more than you know. But you can't fix this, Lucky, and you can't fix me."

"I understand." She squeezed my hand. "But there's a girl in there who could be a part of that process. And I don't want you to miss out on that because of your demons."

"You're not going to give up are you?" I shook my head exasperated.

"No, I'm not. Not with that and not about anything else. Tell Zane the truth, please, Noah." She whispered up to me. "It won't break him. I promise you. He deserves to know. He's hurting more now then you'll ever know."

"You don't know everything, Lucky." I looked at her with a strained expression. "There's more to the story."

"Tell him, Noah." She said firmly. "It's not up to you to protect him."

"He's my brother. That's my job." I argued.

"No, Noah. Your job is to love him and to be honest with him. Always. No matter how hard or difficult it is. You need to be honest with him. You can't shield him from the truth." She took a deep breath. "Because the truth always has a habit of getting out. And you don't want him to find out from someone else, do you?"

I shook my head and I realized that she was correct. There was no way that I was going to be able to keep this a secret from Zane forever. He would find out eventually, and if he found out from someone else, he would resent me forever. I knew Lucky was right. I had to tell him. Even if that meant breaking him down again. I hated to do it, but I knew that our relationship would never be without a strain if I didn't come clean.

"Hey, you two." Sidney opened the door and waved us in. "I wasn't sure if you were going to make it in."

"I was just talking to Noah. Sorry, Sidney." She gave him a quick kiss on the cheek. "How are you?"

"Good. Your lovely fiancée and his friend are inside." Sidney grinned and closed the door behind us. "Though, I think she may be more of Noah's friend, yes?"

"You're so astute, Sidney." Lucky smiled at him and they walked arm-in-arm. I took a deep breath to steady the nerves that had suddenly hit me. I suddenly had nerves in my stomach and I realized that I was excited to see Robin.

"Hey, Noah." Betty rushed over to me and gave me a hug. "I just can't get over seeing you."

"I missed you as well, Betty."

"Boy, do you know how many tears I shed for you?" She shook her head and shuddered. "But all's well that ends well."

"Yes." I smiled at her warmly and gave her cheek a big kiss. I felt the hairs on the back of my neck rise as I heard footsteps walk into the room. I turned around slowly and saw Robin standing there, looking at me shyly. "Hi."

"Hi," she responded back and gave me a quick smile.

"It's good to see you."

"You, too." Her eyes searched mine, and before I knew what I was doing I had stepped towards her, brought her into my arms, and given her a kiss on the lips. "Why, hello to you, too," she laughed, flushing a little.

"I hope that was okay."

"It was more than okay." She giggled and touched her lips quickly. "You taste like chocolate."

"Good taste buds." I smiled. "I had a hot chocolate before I got here. Lucky gave me one before we left the house to calm down my nerves."

"That doesn't sound too good." She looked at me curiously.

"It's not that good." I sighed. "But I'm better now. How did your audition go?" I changed the subject and she shook her head and made a face.

"Let's just say I'm not interested in dying my hair purple and getting 48DDD implants for a role."

"You're not?" I laughed, and turned around when I realized that everyone in the room was staring at us.

"Hey, bro." Zane winked at me. "Maybe you can save the chat-up lines for tonight."

"I'm not …" I glared at him. "What are you doing here anyway?"

"I came to see what's going on with the documentary." He shrugged. "Plus, I had a special delivery to make. You can thank me later."

"Thanks, Santa Claus." I rolled my eyes and then turned to Robin quickly. "Not that I'm saying you're my present or anything. Trust me, I am not objectifying you."

"Uh, thanks, I guess." She laughed and made a face. "I know you most probably think I'm crazy and quick to ignite, but I'm really not like fireworks. You don't have to be that careful around me."

"I think I'd rather be more careful than not right now." I smiled.

"Fair enough."

"So would anyone like tea and cookies?" Betty picked up her teapot. "I just boiled some water, so it should still be hot."

"Betty, get the kids some Cokes. Not everyone wants tea." Sidney responded to her, and she glared at him.

"I'll have some tea, thanks Betty."

"Of course you would, Noah." Sidney smiled at me. "Let's all go sit down. I've got old bones, you know."

"You've got old everything, Sidney Johnson." Betty handed me a plate of cookies. "Let the children relax for a moment before you have them working."

"It's okay." I grinned at her. "I'm pretty excited to talk about what I've been working on." I followed Sidney to the couch and sat down. He leaned over to me and gave me a stern look. "You told your brother the truth yet?"

"No." I shook my head. "Soon."

"I still got them papers." He sat back. "You let me know when you want them."

"I'll let you know," I nodded.

"So who's the girl?" Sidney continued and nodded towards Robin, who was standing next to Lucky and laughing at something. "She's real pretty."

"She's just a friend."

"Seems like more than a friend to me." He looked down at his wedding ring. "I mean, I've only been married for a few hundred years. I don't know much about love and them things."

"Sidney." I admonished him. "I don't love her." I hissed quietly to make sure no one else could hear us. "I barely know her. We barely went on one quasi-date."

"She gets to you though." He looked at me thoughtfully. "You get to her as well."

"She's fragile." I sighed.

"Yes. I'm glad you see it. She has a hard exterior. But it's a shell that's easily broken. She's got a story, that one. Be careful not to break her heart."

"I would never do that," I retorted, angry that he thought I was capable of such a thing.

"You need to finish your business off in Palm Bonita before you start dating anyone new." He stared into my eyes seriously. "That's some serious business you're involved in, Noah. You got to be careful."

"I am being careful." I sighed. "Did you speak to your son?"

"Yes." He nodded. "He's a family attorney in Illinois, though. He said he's not that familiar with the family court system in Florida."

"But did he have any advice?" I looked at him bleakly. I had called Sidney earlier in the week and filled him in on the situation with Skylar because I had needed to talk to someone about it. I felt guilty for not telling Zane, but I just wasn't ready to tell him about everything without going into what had happened with Mom.

"He said that you should just give it up. You're never going to get her. She's never going to be yours." Sidney looked at me bleakly. "He said that it's admirable how much you love her, but you can't change the facts."

"So he thinks I should just give up?" I was angry. "She was counting on me."

"You aren't God, Noah. You can't make miracles happen."

"I can try."

"And that's why I love you, son." He nodded approvingly. "You don't give up, no matter how difficult the odds. The world needs more men like you."

"I haven't done anything yet."

"You have a pure heart." He patted my back. "That's enough."

"I'm going to tell Zane." I blurted out, changing the subject. "I think I'm going to tell him. He has a right to know."

"That's what I've been telling you."

"He's going to be devastated." I closed my eyes.

"He's still got a wonderful family." Sidney's eyes blazed. "We're all still one big family."

"I know." I smiled at him gratefully. "You're the granddad we never had."

"Do you want me to be there when you tell him?"

"No." I shook my head. "I need to do this alone."

"Take him into my study." Sidney nodded as if thinking. "The file you gave me is in my desk, second drawer from the right."

"I don't know if I should show him." I paused. "I was just going to tell him about Mom."

"Tell him everything, Noah. Don't keep it in anymore."

"Okay." I jumped up and hurried over to Zane. "Hey, bro. Do you think we can talk for a moment?"

"Uh, sure?" He looked at me quizzically and I glanced at Lucky, who nodded at me with a quick smile.

"Sidney said we can go in his study."

"Okay, then." He put down his cup and saucer and followed me to the study. I closed the door behind him and we both took a seat. "What's this about, then? You're not upset because I brought Robin, are you? I told Lucky I didn't think it was a good idea."

"No, I'm not upset." I smiled at him gently. "I'm glad you brought her. She's a nice girl, and maybe we can start over again. From the beginning."

"I didn't know that you needed to start over." He gave me a look. "Or are you being overly dramatic?"

"I want to talk to you about Mom." I cut him off, no longer interested in small talk.

"Oh," his face turned serious as he realized the gravity of our conversation.

"Before I went to Palm Bonita, I hired a private detective. I wanted help trying to find out what happened with Mom."

"You never could give it up." He laughed, but the lightness didn't reach his eyes. His shoulders looked tense and I could see the strain in his face.

"Yeah. I couldn't." I sighed. "I always was a glutton for punishment."

"So, you hired a detective?"

"Yeah." I nodded. "I gave him all the information I had, which wasn't much, but he was able to find some leads. You see, she was in the system."

"She was a criminal?" Zane looked shocked.

"No, she was in the immigration system. She applied for a visa when she moved to the States."

"She wasn't American?" Zane sat back in confusion.

"No. She was, or rather is, from France. She moved to the States to be an au pair. She was interested in being an actress as well, so that's why she chose California. She thought she'd meet some hot actor or director and get into movies."

"Oh." He frowned. "How do you know this?"

"Sorry, I'm skipping ahead. So I hired the detective, and he found her in a couple of databases. He saw the visa application and some sealed mental records."

"Mental records?"

"I mean patient records from a mental institute."

"She was in a mental institute?" Zane's eyes were wide. "Oh, God, don't tell me we inherited some crazy gene from her. That's all I need."

"No." I shook my head. "I think she suffered from depression, maybe bipolar as well. I don't really know."

"So she left us because she was depressed?"

"No." I shook my head. "She had postpartum depression and she was scared she was going to harm us. I think she was close to a nervous breakdown. And, well, it didn't help that she was with Dad."

"I suppose not." Zane ran his fingers through his hair. "I always wondered if she was depressed or something. I guess I never realized that would make someone leave her two sons. So the detective told you all this?"

"No, he gave me the contact information to a man she had listed on her visa application in France. Turns out that she had listed her father on the application and he still lived at that address."

"How do you know?" He frowned at me. "Oh, is that when you went back to France?"

"Yes." I nodded. "I tried to talk to you about it all, but you just weren't interested and I didn't want to force the conversation until I knew exactly what had happened. I was so excited, you know. I thought I was going to be able to arrange this happy family reunion."

"That didn't exactly work out." Zane gave me a wry smile.

"Yeah, it didn't." I sighed. "But everything went crazy all at once. I went to Mexico on that weekend trip with Angelique and Braydon, and I called the FBI, and then I went on another trip to France and I met her and my brain was inundated with too much information. I was mad, and sad, and angry and scared and I didn't know if I was coming or going."

"So you just disappeared without saying anything." Zane looked at me with an angry expression. "I never thought you were one to just run away."

"I thought I was protecting you." I sighed. "I don't know why—"

"Why did she pretend she didn't know me?" Zane cut me off. "And why does she still call you? It doesn't make sense to me."

"She's not your mom." I spurted it out and waited for him to explode.

"What are you talking about?" Zane frowned. "Of course she's my mom. If she's your mom, she's my mom. We're brothers, duh."

"She's not your biological mom, Zane." I stared into his eyes and he stared back at me with a wild expression. "She was your au pair when you were a baby. She slept with Dad, and they started a relationship. As much as he could be in a relationship. And then she got pregnant with me and she thought she'd made it. But he still treated her like the au pair."

"Who's my mom, then?" Zane looked like a zombie as he spoke slowly. "Where's my mom?"

I took a deep breath before I continued. This was the part I was dreading the most. "She's dead, Zane. She died from complications during childbirth."

"You mean my childbirth?" Zane looked dazed. "She died because she had me?" He sat back and closed his eyes, his fists clenched and I could see his chest heaving up and down.

"It wasn't your fault, Zane. I saw the records. She had a pre-existing condition that the doctors missed. She would have died whether she had had you or not."

"I killed my mother. And you're not my brother." He started laughing hysterically. "Any other surprises for me? Am I really from Pluto? Are you going to tell me that Lucky is a figment of my imagination as well?"

"Zane." I said his name loudly and with authority. "Please. I didn't want to tell you because I was scared you would lose it. But you can't lose it, Zane. None of this is your fault."

"How could you not tell me, Noah?" He jumped up from his chair. "How could you keep this from me?"

"I was scared." I jumped up as well. "I didn't want you to be hurt. I didn't want you to take it the wrong way."

"Take what the wrong way? I mean, why would I take it the wrong way? I'm not who I thought I am. My whole life has been a lie." He paced back and forth. "I don't even know who I am."

"You know you're still my big brother." I said slowly. "You know you're still the guy that went out of his way to find out what happened to me, and you dated a billion girls to seek revenge for my murder. You're still the guy that promised me that you'd be by my side every day of my life. Remember that day when we pretended to camp in the backyard and you told me that as long as we both lived, I'd always have you?"

"I think I remember saying something about us being the same because we had the exact same blood running through our veins as well. And that was a lie." He turned away from me. "I don't even know who half of my bloodline belongs to. I don't even know who I really am."

"Blood didn't make us a family, Zane. *We* made us a family. Our love and undying affection and care for each other make us a family. The fact that we would do anything for each other makes us a family. You're still my brother, Zane. My full brother. I don't care if we only share half a bloodline." My voice rose as I talked to him, and he turned to look at me with tears in his eyes.

"I'm sorry." He nodded. "I didn't mean to imply anything else."

"I have something for you." I walked over to Sidney's file cabinet and opened the second drawer and pulled out a folder and handed it to Zane. "This is for you." I watched as he opened it slowly with a weary expression. "It's everything I could find out about your birth mom and her family."

"Oh." He sat back down again with the folder in his lap and held it in his hands gingerly.

"Your grandfather died in World War II. He was a war hero." I started talking when I realized that Zane was too dazed to look at the file himself. "And your grandmother was a nurse. She never remarried. She brought your mom up by herself, even supported her through college. Your mom was a teacher." He looked up at me, and I could see tears in his eyes as I spoke. "She taught kindergarteners. She loved them and they loved her. There are two class photos in the folder. You can see what she looked like. She was beautiful. She was older than Dad by eleven years." Zane's eyes widened in surprise and I laughed. "I know. I was shocked as well."

"She was older than Dad?" Zane spoke finally and opened the folder. I watched as he went through the papers and photographs eagerly, holding them carefully and studying them intently. "She was beautiful." He stared at one of the photos and smiled at me. "She looks like she was a loving woman. Like she would have made a good mother."

"She was really excited to have you." I continued on. "The detective found many people who worked with her. They all said she was so excited to have a baby of her own. She boasted to everyone that she was going to call him Zane because he was her strong little man. She used to tell everyone that when you kicked she thought you were going to break through her stomach."

"That's not what hurt her, is it?" Zane's expression turned bleak again and I almost cursed myself out.

"No, that's not why. She loved you so much, Zane. You were the child she had been waiting for her whole life." I took a deep breath and continued. "She chose your life instead of her own."

"What?" Zane looked confused.

"When she went into labor, the doctors told her they could try and save her or they could try and save you. And she didn't hesitate. She chose you." I took a deep breath. "And there's supposed to be a letter."

"A letter?"

"I don't know where it is." I gave him an apologetic look. "I don't even know if it's true, but the detective spoke to someone that worked at the hospital when she died. She was a receptionist or something. She said that your mom left you a letter."

"Why didn't you tell me any of this before, Noah?"

"Because I was scared of how you would react." I answered honestly. "You were in a bad, bitter place, bro. I wasn't sure that you'd be able to handle it all."

"I understand." He gave me a small smile. "I was in a bad place. But now that I have Lucky, I feel like nothing can phase me. I'm really hurt and upset, but I understand your reasons for keeping it secret, Noah."

"I love you, Zane."

"I love you too, bro." He stood up and gave me a big bear hug before pulling back. "And now, if you'll excuse me. I want to go and find Lucky and tell her everything." He laughed as he shook his head. "I can't believe that I've become that guy."

I laughed as well and agreed with him. "I can't believe it either."

CHAPTER TEN

"*I WANT TO GO TO ARUBA.*" *She sat at the table and looked up at me with a demanding face.*

"*I can't leave Palm Bonita,*" *I sighed, irritated that we were having this conversation again.*

"*I want to go on vacation. This shit is boring.*" *She looked at me, annoyed. "No one in Aruba is going to know or care who you are.*"

"*I'm sorry, but I can't go.*"

"*What use are you to me?*"

"I thought you liked my company." I turned away from her, unable to look at her. I wasn't sure who she was becoming, or maybe I just hadn't known who she really was when we first started dating.

"Noah, it's not that I don't like your company. It's that I'll like it more if we went to Aruba." She continued painting her fingernails and held them up to me. "What do you think?" I stared at the bright red polish on her nails and thought the color was apt. Her fingers looked like they had been dipped in blood and really, that was the way I was starting to think of her. She was a bloodsucker, only interested in her own needs. The fact was I would have already dumped her if there weren't other issues to consider, other circumstances that made it more difficult. It was hard for me to walk away from her when I knew that I was possibly putting someone else at risk.

"Looks good." I faked a smile and turned away. "If you're wanting to be a prostitute or vampire." I said under my breath.

"What's that?" Her voice was shrill, and I looked over at her with a blank expression.

"What's what?"

"What did you just say?" Her eyes narrowed at me coldly and I almost shivered as I stared at her. There was no happiness or joy in her spirit. She looked broken. Broken and distant.

"Nothing, just that I wished I could take you to Aruba."

"Whatever." She flung her hair over her shoulders. "I'll figure out a way myself or with the help of someone else."

"What do you mean?" I frowned. "You're not going to steal again?"

"You act like that's a bad thing." She stood up and walked over to me. "You act like you didn't get off fucking me in that stranger's house after we stole the handbag."

"We didn't steal anything." I took a step away from her, feeling my body temperature rising. It was getting harder and harder for me to disguise my feelings.

"No one would believe that you weren't in it with me. Were you not in the house with me?" She laughed cattily, and ran her index finger all the way down my chest and to my crotch, which sat motionless. She looked up at me with a pout. "There was a day when all I had to do was touch you and you would rise to attention."

"I'm not in the mood." I looked away from her.

"Do you not find me attractive anymore?" Her tone changed to one of pity and hurt, and I looked over at her. She looked distraught, but I wasn't sure if it was because she was genuinely sad that I was pulling away from her or just because her feminine wiles won't working.

"You're beautiful." I stared at her and answered honestly.

"I don't mean to be like this, you know." Her eyes were open and held a touch of bleakness. "I've just been through so much in my life. Every day I'm just in survival mode. I'm just trying to get by. I just want to be free." Tears slid from her eyes. "I just want to get out of here and be free."

"I know you do." I held her hand and squeezed it compassionately, and for one moment we were once again united in our grief.

"I hope that today hasn't been filled with too many bombshells," I grimaced as I got into the car with Robin. "I bet you're wishing that you didn't come over to the Johnsons' today."

"Not at all," she laughed. "Though it has been one of those *Days of Our Lives* types of day."

"That's a lot of family information for you to get at one time." I couldn't stop myself from laughing as we pulled out of the Johnsons' driveway. "I wouldn't be surprised if you never wanted to see me again."

"If that's all you've got, then your life is nothing compared to mine." She grinned at me, but I saw a tinge of truth and sadness in her eyes. "But, just to clear things up: no, I do not want to not see you again. I'm actually glad that Zane and Lucky intervened."

"So am I," I laughed again. "Though do not tell them that. I don't want them thinking that they can try to dictate my life, but they definitely helped me here. Especially after the other night."

"What happened there?" She looked over at me curiously.

"I'm not sure." I looked at her. "I got the feeling that we both weren't ready to be in a certain place."

"Yeah, perhaps." She sat back and looked out the window. "I guess we're both treading water here."

"Would you like to go to a movie with me?" I blurted out before I could think about it too much. "I can also just take you home if you prefer."

"What about your brother? Don't you want to be with him?"

"I think he'd rather be with Lucky right now." I smiled at her, happy to see that she was the kind of woman who thought about others before herself. "I'm sure we'll be doing more talking tomorrow. Once he has time to get over the initial shock, I'm pretty sure he will have a lot more questions."

"That was brave of you to tell him at the Johnsons'." Her voice was light and non-judgmental, which I appreciated. "Weren't you worried he would just lose it and go off on you?"

"Yes," I laughed, "but Sidney is like my family. He's known pretty much everything. He was the one who helped me find the private detective. He's the one who has been badgering me to tell Zane. I know this sounds crazy, but I always knew I wanted Sidney to be around when I told Zane. He's like my support system. Do I sound like a total weirdo to you right now?"

"No, of course not." She reached over and squeezed my arm. "He seems really nice and so does his wife. Before you and Lucky arrived, I was talking to them and they really showed a genuine interest in me. It was like they knew exactly what to say to make me feel better about myself."

"It's a gift that they have." I smiled at her warmly, glad that she had taken to them both. "It's like they can see into your soul and the worries that you have, and they soothe you with their words and care."

"Yes," she nodded. "When Sidney spoke to me, I felt like he knew where I was coming from and what my dreams and obstacles were. It was funny." Her voice grew low. "It's hard to meet people who genuinely care about you like that. Who want to know your story, rather than just talk about themselves."

"Yes, yes, it is."

"So, you were in witness protection?" She changed the subject. "How did I not know that? That's crazy."

"I wasn't technically in witness protection." I laughed. "But yes, I was helping the FBI and the DEA with a case and I had to disappear."

"Okay, I take back my earlier statement. Your life isn't like *Days of our Lives*, it's more like *Mission Impossible*."

"Not really. All I had to do was go hide out in a small town in Florida. It was Zane who was actually getting to the bottom of the case."

"That must have been hard, though, leaving your family."

"It was one of the hardest things I've ever had to do in my life." I found myself driving back to Zane's house instead of the movie. "The day I realized that I had to fake my own suicide and have my brother believe I was dead is still surreal to me."

"What made you go along with it?"

"The agent who was in charge of the case told me that unless I complied, it was likely that they would come after me and my family, which, honestly, I doubted. But then he said, 'Think of all the other innocent lives you could be saving. The lives that get caught in the crossfire. They were drug dealers, they didn't care who they hurt.' And that's when I knew I had to do it. Special Agent Waldron had shown me photographs of many of the people that they believed were killed by the cartel and there were over twenty children. I didn't want there to be any new faces added to that pile."

"Wow." Robin's eyes widened. "You're really selfless. Now you make me feel bad for going off on you two times."

"I just did what anyone with a conscience would have done." I shrugged. "And I'm pretty sure you will go off on me again, at some point. I can be infuriating, just ask Zane." I laughed.

"Where are we going?" She looked out the window as she laughed.

"I figured we could watch a movie." I paused. "But at home, if that's not too presumptuous. You didn't answer earlier and so I thought this may be nice. We can relax, have a few laughs and be comfortable."

"Sounds good to me." She gave me a wide smile. "Are you sure we won't be bothering Zane and Lucky?"

"Well, here's the other part." I made a face at her. "I was hoping we could watch it in my room? I know what you're thinking, but it's not because I want to sleep with you. I have a king-sized bed so we won't even have to touch. I just figured it will give us more privacy if they are already home, or if they come home while we are still watching it."

"Don't worry, Noah." She giggled. "I understand."

"Phew." I pulled into the driveway. "I didn't want you thinking this was another seduction move. And that all I wanted from you was a night of hot sex."

"Don't remind me of that last conversation." She groaned. "I'm surprised you don't think I'm bipolar."

"You're not?" I feigned surprise and she hit me in the shoulder before we both jumped out of the car.

"Funny." She laughed. "Though I suppose I deserve that."

"Let's go inside." I walked over to her side of the car and grabbed her hand. As we touched, I felt another spark jolt through me and I smiled to myself knowing that the connection I had witnessed previously was still there.

"So, are you going to tell me more about your time in Florida? Where did you go?" Robin looked up at me with a happy face, and I felt my heart start to pound. How could I tell her about everything that had happened in Palm Bonita? It was all so complicated and heartbreaking. I didn't want to burden her with all that information. Not in the same day she had found out about all my family drama. It almost seemed too much. I didn't want to lose her right when I was getting to know her because of an information overload. Not when I was finally getting a do-over with her. Plus, I didn't know how to tell her about Skylar. I didn't know if she would understand.

"There's not really much to tell." I said smoothly. "I stayed in a small town called Palm Bonita and basically just sat around and waited until I was able to come home."

"Oh, that sucks." She gave my upper arm a squeeze. "That must have been so boring. Did you make any friends?"

"Not really." I shook my head. "I kept to myself most of the time."

"Aww, that's awful. What were the people like? Did they ask you where you came from?" Her eyes were excited. "I bet they were all curious as to who you were."

"Not really." Which was true. The people in Palm Bonita didn't ask questions because they didn't want anyone to ask them anything, either.

"So what did you do?" She looked confused. "Just sat and watched TV?"

"I did a lot of TV watching." I nodded. "Not much else. I didn't really have any friends, so I was by myself quite a bit."

"So," she paused. "No special lady friends?" Her eyes looked into mine questioningly, and my stomach churned.

"Not really." I lied, feeling horrible as I did so. But I knew that Robin didn't want to know about my relationship in Palm Bonita. She didn't want to hear about all the places we had sex and how I lost myself in the relationship because I fell in love.

"Oh, wow." She laughed. "Sorry for the twenty questions."

"That's okay. What about you? When did you last date?" I asked her, honestly wanting to know the answer but also wanting to take the focus of the conversation away from myself.

"Right before I moved to Los Angeles." She gave me a weak smile. "What movie are we going to watch?"

She walked away from me and looked at some of the pictures Zane had up on the wall. "These are cool."

"Yeah," I nodded. "They were painted by kids with cancer."

"Oh, that's sad."

"Cancer is a horrible disease." I agreed. "Zane does everything he can to support cancer research. He gives a lot of money to a lot of different hospitals." I paused. "But honestly, I think the best part is that he goes and he visits the kids and he talks to them and plays with them, and he supports their visions for the future."

"Wow, that's amazing."

"Yeah. He's pretty cool." I nodded and I felt warm inside as I once again realized how blessed I was to have him as a brother.

"Want anything to eat or drink before we go upstairs?"

"Do you have any wine?" She laughed. "Or chocolate?"

"I think we have both. And strawberries, if you want some."

"That sounds delicious." She followed me into the kitchen and I handed her two wine glasses and a box of Quality Street that I found in the cupboard. Zane had an addiction to English chocolates and always ordered the boxes in bulk. I grabbed a wine bottle, opener, and some strawberries from the fridge.

"Okay, we'll all set. Let's go feast." Robin followed me up the stairs and into my bedroom, and we placed all the goodies on the nightstand next to my bed. "Feel free to take your shoes off and relax." I smiled at her as she just stood there. She smiled back at me and slipped her shoes off and pulled off her sweater. I stood there staring at her torso as she straightened her clothes, and I tried to avoid staring at her breasts as they beckoned to me through her thin tank top.

"I guess we'll be sitting on the bed?" She gave me a wry smile as she slid onto the bed and leaned back against the headboard.

"Yes, you look comfortable." I opened the bottle of wine and stared at her as she lay back.

"It's a comfortable bed." She smiled at me. "I've missed being on a comfortable bed."

"Feel free to sleep in mine anytime you like." I groaned as soon as I realized what I had said. "And I mean sleep, not sex or anything."

"You're going to make me think I've grown warts or something." She laughed self-consciously. "You keep telling me you're not interested in sleeping with me."

"Oh, don't think that. I'd love to sleep with you." I paused. "I mean, when you're ready. When the time is ready. I don't need to sleep with you anytime soon."

"Okay." She patted the spot next to her on the bed. "I appreciate it. Now where's my wine and chocolate?"

"A little demanding, aren't we?" I laughed and handed her a glass before sitting down next to her and opening the box of chocolates. "Here we go."

"Oh, I've never had these before. Are they good?"

"Are they good? Is this a joke?" I looked at her with wide eyes. "Why, Quality Street are on the best chocolates in the world."

"In the world, eh?" She leaned towards me and I could see her pupils dilate as our thighs touched.

"Yes, the best in the world." I reached into the box and pulled out a pink wrapper. "Try this one first, it's my favorite."

"What is it?"

"Fudge covered with a light layer of milk chocolate."

"Oh, my, that sounds divine."

"It is." I opened the wrapper and took a small bite. "Sorry, I couldn't resist." I grinned as I chewed on the sweet in my mouth. "Here you go." I lifted my hand to her mouth and fed her the other half of the chocolate. She opened her mouth and ate the chocolate slowly, her eyes light as she enjoyed the sweet.

"That was good." She nodded. "Very good."

"Wasn't it just?" I leaned in towards her and licked off a chocolate crumb that was stuck to her lower lip. "I like how it tastes on you better." I sucked on her lower lip and she moaned before moving in closer to me and crushing her lips to mine. Her tongue slipped into my mouth and I sucked on it, enjoying the taste of chocolate in her mouth. I kissed her back hard and she pulled away from me quickly. I sat back quickly, worried

I had messed up again, but she absolved my fears quickly.

"Glass of wine still in my hand," she gasped and placed the glass down on the nightstand.

"Oops." I laughed as I realized I was also holding my glass and that some wine had spilled on the bed. I leaned over and placed my glass down next to hers and then lay back down. "Shall we watch a movie now?"

"Sure," she nodded and lay back next to me. Her body was aligned directly next to mine, and our entire sides were touching. I could see her bosom moving up and down, and I could also see the lower part of her stomach as her top had ridden up a little bit. It was all I could do to not reach my hand down to caress her stomach and then her breasts.

"What movies do you like?" I asked casually, trying to calm myself down.

"Honestly, I love thrillers." She turned over on her side to face me. "I know most men expect all women to love romance, but I love thrillers."

"Thrillers are great. What's your favorite?"

"*Primal Fear*," she answered right away. "I love both Richard Gere and Edward Norton, and I think they were both so great in that movie."

"I think I vaguely remember it." I laughed.

"It's great. You need to watch it."

"I suppose we could watch it now? I can see if it's on Netflix."

"No." She shook her head. "I don't think so."

"Oh? Why not?" I asked surprised.

"Well, when you watch it, I want you to be see the whole thing." She laughed.

"Huh?" I was confused.

"I don't think we'll get to the end of the movie." She ran her fingers down my chest. "And I don't want you to miss the end. It's too good a movie."

"Oh." My heart thudded at her words and I felt my erection growing as her fingers continued their quest along my upper torso.

"Unless of course, you think you'll be able to see the whole movie?"

"I can't say that I would make it happen." I answered honestly and reached over and traced the line around her belly button. She shivered slightly at my touch and I reached my hand up under her tank top and caressed her stomach before working my way up to her bra. I watched her face carefully to make sure that she wasn't uncomfortable with where everything was going. She smiled at me and moved in closer to me, before moving her hand underneath my shirt and rubbing the hair on my chest.

"It's so silky." She breathed out and then gasped as my fingers cradled her right breast over her bra.

"Thank you." I leaned in and kissed her again. She pulled away from me slightly, paused for a moment, and then pulled her tank top off. I stared at her beautiful body and then pulled my shirt off. We both just sat there for a moment gazing at each other, and then I reached over and slid one of her bra straps down. She lay there motionless and watched me slide the other bra strap down. I then reached behind her and undid the clasp, and the bra fell onto the bed. I was unable to keep my hands off of her, so I reached over and squeezed her breasts into my hand, molding them to my palm before softly pinching her nipples. She closed her eyes and a soft moan escaped her mouth as I teased her hardened buds. I reached over and took her left nipple into my mouth and suckled on it while my right hand played with her other nipple.

"Oh, Noah," she gasped as my teeth nibbled on her. She lay flat on the bed and opened her legs slightly.

"Yes, ma'am?" I grinned down at her mischievously and kissed in the valley between her breasts before allowing my tongue to explore the line right down to her belly button. I kissed my way to the top of her pants before pausing to look up at her to make sure it was okay to proceed.

"I guess we're not going to be starting the movie anytime soon." She gave me a sly smile and wiggled her bottom on the bed. I took that as my sign to proceed and slowly undid her pants and slid them down her legs. She was wearing a pair of black lacy underwear, and I lowered my lips to her ankle and kissed up her calf and then to her inner thigh. She spread her legs and I continued kissing up her inner thigh until my lips were at the center of her. She squirmed beneath me and I suckled on her bud through her underwear. I could smell and taste her wanton lust, and it made me feel delirious with power and hornier than ever. I kissed up to the top of her panties and started pulling them down with my teeth. She lifted her bottom off of the bed to make it easier for me to slide them off, and I used my hands by the time I had pulled them to the top of her thigh because I was too impatient to wait any longer to get them off. Before she knew what was happening, my mouth was back in the midst of her womanhood, and I explored her eagerly with my tongue before sucking on her throbbing bud. She squirmed beneath me as she grew wet, and I felt her orgasm as soon as I slid my tongue inside of her.

"Oh, Noah!" She screamed as my tongue slid in and out of her and I felt her hands in my hair pushing my face closer to her sex so that she could feel me deeper inside of her. I licked her eagerly and passionately, enjoying the feel of her writhing sex against my face. I could feel my erection pushing against my pants almost uncomfortably, and I was eager to feel a release soon myself.

"Yes, Robin." I grinned as I kissed my way back up to her lips. She wrapped her legs around me as I kissed her passionately, allowing her to taste her own juices. She reached down and unbuckled my pants, and I jumped up and pulled them and my boxers off quickly. She gasped as she stared at my erection, hard and proud, jutting out at her. I was proud of my penis and fell back onto the bed next to her, allowing my hardness to rub up roughly against her inner thigh and close to her opening. She rolled me over so that she was lying on top of me. She positioned herself over my hardness and started moving back and forward without allowing me to enter her. I groaned as she teased me with her grind and pulled her down towards me so that I could play with her breasts as she teased me. Our eyes connected and I reached out for her hands so that every part of our body was connected while we teased each over. I groaned as she started moving back and forth on me harder and harder and I grabbed her hips to get her to stop. I knew that I wouldn't be able to stop myself from entering her if she kept up with her grinding.

"Hold on." I groaned as I lifted her off of me and jumped off of the bed. I walked over to my wallet and opened it, praying that I still had some condoms in there. I nearly fainted with relief when I saw two packets and grabbed them quickly. I threw one packet on the nightstand and jumped back on the bed with the other. Robin watched me with a veil of desire clouding her eyes and I quickly opened the packet and slipped the condom on. "Are you sure?" I positioned myself on top of her, not wanting to go ahead unless she was ready.

"I don't know." She bit her lip and looked up at me with a confused expression. "I want to, but it just seems too soon."

I tried not to groan as I collapsed on the bed next to her and gave her a soft smile. "It's okay. We can go at your pace. Like I said before, this isn't about sex for me."

"I know. You're a sweetheart." She turned over to face me and I tried my hardest to keep my eyes on her face and not on her naked body.

"Why, thank you." I reached over and stroked her hair away from her eyes. "You have beautiful eyes, did you know that? They go from green to brown to green, and they haunt me every time I look into them."

"Some people just call them hazel."

"Oh, but they're not just hazel. They're so much more bewitching than just regular hazel." My fingers traced her lips, and she held her breath as I stuck my finger into her mouth. She slowly sucked on it and I groaned as I felt my cock growing hard again. I pulled my finger out of her mouth slowly and lay back again and closed my eyes. "Sorry," I mumbled. "We need to just pause for a moment or I'm going to explode."

"Little Noah, you mean?" She giggled and I felt her breasts against my chest as she leaned into me.

"Who you calling little?" I growled and opened my eyes and pushed her onto her back. "I'll have you know that big Noah is ready to play."

"But I put him in time out." She laughed up at me and I held her hands up by her head. I looked down at her, and my heart caught in my throat as I saw the total innocence and trust in her eyes.

"No one puts Big Noah in the corner." I winked at her, and she groaned.

"Please tell me you are not misquoting *Dirty Dancing.*"

"Or what?" I let go of her wrists and moved my hands down to her breasts, allowing my fingers to gently graze her nipples as I squeezed them.

"Or nothing." She breathed up at me and squirmed beneath me. She then reached up and pulled me down on top of her so that my body was pressed firmly against hers. "Fuck me, Noah."

"Are you sure?" I looked into her eyes to make sure she was not saying the words out of pressure.

"I've never been more sure of anything in my life." She laughed and reached up and grabbed my cock and positioned it between her legs.

"I don't want you to think this is all about sex." I pushed the tip of my cock into her opening and paused. "Are you sure?"

"Oh, my gosh, Noah. Just do it." She moaned and pushed my bottom down and squeezed her legs around my waist so that my cock plunged into her. We both gasped as I slid inside of her, and a spark of electricity passed through us both. I moved slowly at first, loving the feel of her clenched around me. She felt warm and tight, and I had to control myself to stop myself from coming too soon. Robin bucked her hips beneath me and I increased my pace, slamming in and out of her so fast that I could feel my balls bouncing against her with every thrust.

"Touch me," she moaned as I moved in and out of her. Her eyes were blazing with desire. "I need you to touch me at the same time. Please." She groaned and I realized she wanted me to rub her clit as I thrust in and out of her. I adjusted my position so that her legs were up over my shoulders and I reached my thumb down to manually stimulate her as my cock plunged into her.

"Oh, yes. Oh, my God, yes!" she screamed and closed her eyes as I felt my climax building up and I rubbed her clit harder so that I could ensure I didn't come before her. "Oh, Noah!" she screamed out loud and her eyes popped open as she started climaxing. Her body wiggled against me and across the sheets, and her breasts bounced up and down as she gyrated against me.

She screamed as she came and I plunged into her hard two more times before I exploded inside of her. We stared at each other as we climaxed together and I collapsed on top of her, my cock still inside of her as we both finished at the same time. I gave her a long hard kiss and rolled onto my side. I quickly pulled off the condom and threw into the trashcan on the other side of the bed.

"You're amazing." I leaned over and pulled Robin into my arms. "That was amazing."

"Thank you." She looked up at me apprehensively. "I don't know what to say. I've never orgasmed like that before."

"Really?" I grinned, happy at her admission.

"Really." She laughed. "I think I would have come even if you hadn't rubbed my clit."

"Do you need to be touched to come?" I cocked my head to the side and ran my fingers down her stomach to her pussy.

"Yes. Well, I've never come without manual stimulation as well."

"Oh. That's sad." I reached down and rubbed her clit and she moaned.

"Oh, don't." She squealed and tightened her legs against my hand. "I'm not sure I can handle another orgasm again so soon."

"Oh?" I laughed and slipped a finger inside of her. "Are you sure?"

"Noah," she closed her eyes. "You're the devil, you know that?"

"No." I removed my finger and watched her stare at me with wide eyes as I put it into my mouth and sucked it. "You taste amazing."

"I can't believe you're growing hard again already." She looked down at my cock, which was already growing rigid again, and placed her fingers around the shaft. "I didn't expect you to be so well endowed."

"Was I too big for you?" I raised an eyebrow at her and she laughed.

"No." She shook her head. "It felt just right."

"Yes, it did." I groaned as I felt her fingers moving up and down the length of me. "Don't start something you can't continue."

"Or?" She stopped and rolled over back onto her back. "What?"

"You are not going to just leave me hanging here, are you?" I groaned. "Big Noah is ready to play again."

"Well, little Robin needs a longer break." She laughed.

"What about back door Robin?"

"Back door?" She looked confused and then she shook her head at me. "Really?"

"Have you ever done it?" I grinned at her. "You shouldn't knock what you don't know."

"Actually, I tried it once. And I wasn't a huge fan."

"He most probably didn't know what he was doing."

"And you do?"

"I just gave you the best orgasm of your life, right?"

"I never said that." She blushed and I laughed as I reached down and nibbled on her nipple while allowing my fingers to play with her other nipple.

"I think you pretty much did." I smirked at her. "But that's okay, that was pretty much the best orgasm I've ever had as well."

"Really?" She looked surprised. "And what do you mean pretty much?"

"Well, I only orgasmed once, so I can't be sure." I laughed as she pushed me onto my back and rolled over on top of me.

"Well, I guess I'll have to prove it to you." She looked down at me with glossy eyes, and I laughed as she trailed her breasts along my face and allowed her nipples to brush against my lips. I tried to catch one in my mouth, but she moved it away quickly.

"Oh, no you don't. I'm in control now." She sat back and shifted positions so that she was straddling me.

"I love a woman in charge."

"Really?" She traced her fingers along my nipples and squeezed them hard before moving her fingers back down to my stomach.

"Yes." I laughed and lay back, happy to allow her to take me on her sexual journey.

"Good." She moved forward and then shifted backwards quickly and before I knew what was going on, I felt my cock sliding inside of her.

"Oh." I reached over to the nightstand to grab the other condom, but she shook her head.

"It's okay. I'm on the pill." She slowly moved back and forth on me, and the sensation of her bare skin against mine made me grow harder even faster. "I want to feel all of you inside of me."

"Fuck." My body tensed as she bounced up and down on me and swiveled her hips back and forth. She was moving so quickly that I was sliding in and out of her effortlessly. I could feel every sensation even more deeply as she moved up and down. I felt my cock going so deeply into her that I almost felt that she was becoming a part of me. I knew that I was also hitting the right spot because she had closed her eyes and was moaning as she increased her pace. Her hair was flying everywhere and her breasts were bouncing up and down with abandon as she rode me. I reached up and squeezed her nipples as she rode me and I felt her climax a few seconds later. This time she increased her pace, and I found myself climaxing into her a few seconds later. She collapsed on top of me, and I grabbed her face and kissed her hard.

"You proved your point." I muttered against her lips. "That was the best orgasm of my life."

"You proved your point as well," she whispered against my lips. "That was my first orgasm from penetration alone."

"There are plenty more where that came from." I drew her hair away from her face and stared up into her face. "You're so beautiful, Robin."

"You're not bad yourself." She rolled over onto her side and grinned. "I'm ready to watch that movie now."

"I'm ready for a quick nap." I laughed and she shook her head.

"Typical man."

"To know us is to love us," I replied quickly, and I laughed as she stuck her tongue out at me. I jumped off of the bed and grabbed the remote control and threw it at her. "Here you go. Feel free to choose a channel. I'm just going to the bathroom. I'll be right back."

"Okay." She smiled and bit her lip.

"Everything okay?"

"Do you have a t-shirt I could wear?" She looked down at her naked body. "I feel a little awkward lying here naked."

"I don't mind you staying naked." I licked my lips and then laughed as she rolled her eyes. "Hold on." I walked to the closet, grabbed a t-shirt, and threw it to her. She caught it and pulled it on quickly.

"Thank you." She smiled and sat back. My breath caught as I stared at Robin and realized which t-shirt I had given her. It was the same t-shirt I had worn all the time in Palm Bonita. It was the same t-shirt that *she* had worn after we made love. I felt my heart thudding as I realized that I was now thinking about *her* while I was with Robin. And I hadn't even told Robin about her. I closed my eyes briefly, not wanting to think of her in this moment. This was a special new beginning for Robin and me. I didn't want the past to ruin us. I had to live in the present now. I had a real future with Robin. I didn't want to mess that up.

"You okay?" Robin looked at me with an anxious look.

"Yeah." I nodded. "Sorry, that t-shirt reminded me of my time in Palm Bonita."

"Oh." She looked down at the graphic of a lone palm tree and the caption 'No man is alone in Palm Bonita.' "Did you get this while you were there?"

"Yeah. A friend gave it to me." I turned around. "I'll be back. I just need to go to the bathroom." I hurried to the bathroom and closed the door and poured some water on my flushed face. "Stupid idiot." I muttered to myself as I pissed. "Why don't you just tell her that she's wearing the t-shirt your ex-girlfriend gave you? The same t-shirt that she used to wear after you fucked her senseless?"

"You okay, Noah?" Robin knocked on the bathroom door, and I froze. How loud had I been?

"Yeah, coming." I washed my hands and walked out of the bathroom and looked at Robin's worried face. "What's wrong?"

"You seem like you got upset." She looked up at me with a concerned face. "I guess you have bad memories about your time in Palm Bonita, huh?"

"I guess," I mumbled, wanting to change the subject but not knowing how.

"What was it like?" She walked back to the bed with me and we sat down. "I understand if you don't want to talk about it, but I'd love to know more about it."

"It was a small town." I sighed and leaned back on the bed. "It was full of criminals. A lot of bad people."

"Wow, how bad were they?"

"Pretty bad." I shrugged. "Murderers, thieves, tax evaders. Anyone who wanted to get away from mainstream society and didn't want to be found moved to Palm Bonita."

"Eww, that sounds horrible. No wonder you have bad memories of the place. Were there any good people?"

"There was one." I started and my eyes lit up at the memory of Skylar. "Out of everyone that I met, there was one person who was an angel with a heart of gold."

"A girl?" Robin's tone was light, but her eyes looked at me with deep interest.

"Yeah. She was my little princess." I stared at Robin and sighed. "She was a beautiful light in that town of darkness."

"I didn't realize that you had someone special there."

"Sorry," I shook my head. "I didn't mean to or want to talk about this. It's not something I like to dwell upon."

"Do you miss her?" Robin's tone sounded jealous, and I felt worry fill me.

"Let's not talk about it." I grabbed her hands. "Let's just think about us." I pulled her against my chest and stroked her head, but all I could think was, 'What if I am successful in bringing Skylar to Los Angeles? What am I going to tell Robin?'

CHAPTER ELEVEN

"WHAT'S YOUR FAVORITE FLAVOR ICE CREAM?" *Skylar grinned at me as she licked her ice cream cone eagerly. "I think mine is chocolate, but I love strawberry cheesecake and mint choc chip as well. Oh, and vanilla." She giggled. "I guess I love a lot of them."*

"I think mine would have to be rum raisin." I smiled at the joy in her eyes, and felt a surge of happiness inside. It was a rare occasion to see her so happy.

"What's rum raisin?"

"It's not a popular flavor." I laughed. "And it's not one you should eat."

"Why not?" She frowned. "I want to try it."

"It's high in alcohol."

"I like alcohol." She licked her lips and I shook my head at her, trying to hide the sorrow in my gaze.

"Alcohol is bad." I grabbed her hand. "Come on, let's go bowling."

"I've never been bowling before." She paused to bite off a big chuck of her wafer cone. "Is it hard?"

"You've never been bowling before?" I forgot to hide my surprise and I saw her react to my statement. She looked a little bit sad and worried and I wanted to slap myself for making her feel bad. "No worries, it's not hard and I can teach you."

"You should be a teacher." She smiled at me, happy again.

"I don't think I would be a good teacher. You're the only one I like teaching."

"That's because I'm your favorite." She nodded happily. "And you're mine."

"I'm glad to hear that."

"You're my most favorite person ever." Skylar's eyes were wide open as she stared at me with her innocent beautiful face. "I never want you to leave."

"I never want to leave, either." I bit my lip and looked away, not knowing how to tell her that one day I was going to have to leave.

"Promise you will never leave me." Her eyes were earnest as she spoke the words so simply.

"I don't know if I can promise that." I paused and looked down at her. "You know I love you very much, but I don't know that I can promise that I'll never leave."

"If you leave, you have to take me with you." She gulped and started breathing fast. "You have to." Tears starting building up in her eyes and they quickly became moist. "You can't leave me here."

"Let's not talk about it now, Skylar." I pulled her towards me and hugged her hard.

"You can't leave me, Noah. Please never leave me. Promise me." She whispered as I held her and I felt my heart freeze over at the sound of her voice pleading with me. I wanted to tell her that I would never leave, but I knew that was one promise I couldn't make.

"You're up early." Lucky walked into the kitchen as I was making coffee. "Early night?"

"Not really." I smiled at her and turned back to the French press. I groaned as I saw Zane walk into the kitchen behind her. He looked me up and down and frowned at my half naked body. All I was wearing was a pair of boxer briefs and I knew he was not happy to see me that way in his kitchen.

"Morning, Noah. Were you hot last night?" Zane gave me a look and I shook my head.

"No, not really."

"What did you do last night?" Lucky spoke up, obviously sensing that Zane was going to continue to go on about my appearance passive aggressively.

"Watched a movie." I grinned, thinking about all the hot sex before and after the movie. "What about you two?"

"Zane and I went down to Santa Monica to an art show, then we had dinner at a new Italian place and talked."

"Are you okay?" I looked at Zane searching to see if he was still upset.

"I'm surprisingly okay." He gave me a reassuring nod. "And don't worry, I'm not mad at you."

"You're not?" I looked over at him in surprise and he laughed.

"Shocker, right?" He shrugged. "I understand why you didn't want to tell me. I don't hold it against you. I most probably wouldn't have told you, either."

"So, we're still brothers?"

"Try getting away from me." He walked over to me and gave me a slap on the shoulder. "Now please pass me a cup of coffee."

"Oh, sorry, I only made enough for two."

"Right? One for me and one for you. Lucky can't have caffeine right now."

"Well, actually the other cup isn't for you."

"Huh?" He looked at me in confusion. "You're going to drink two cups of coffee?"

"No," I shook my head and bit my lip. "The other cup of coffee is for …"

"Me." Robin's voice rang out as she walked into the kitchen looking sexy as hell in just my shirt. "Good morning, everyone." She smiled and looked at me shyly.

"Morning, gorgeous." I walked over and gave her a big kiss. She wrapped her arms around me and kissed me back, pressing her chest against mine. It was at that point that I realized that she was naked underneath the shirt. I turned around and both Zane and Lucky were staring at me with shocked expressions.

"Hey, so Robin stayed over last night." I grinned at both of them and watched as Zane looked at Robin's body appreciatively.

"Hey, can we have a talk, Noah?" Lucky half smiled and half frowned.

"I'm sorry for not asking if I could have a houseguest." I made a face.

"Don't be silly." Lucky shook her head. "This is your home, you can have who you want over."

"We sure don't mind." Zane grinned at me and Lucky hit him in the arm and glared at him. "Don't be jealous, honey."

"I'm not jealous, ass." Lucky blushed, and I felt bad that I may have inadvertently set her green monster off.

"Can we talk after I've had a shower, Lucky?" I walked over to her and gave her a kiss on the cheek.

"Yes." She smiled at me and shook her head before looking over at Robin. "It's good to see you, Robin."

"You too, Lucky." Robin smiled back at her and walked over to me. "Is that coffee ready? I'm about to fall back asleep."

"Well, if the coffee doesn't wake you up. I know something that will."

"Oh, really?" she purred.

"Really." I leaned towards her.

"And what would that be?" She leaned towards me and I felt my body heating up.

"Well, it would consist of …"

"Guys, we are still in the kitchen." Zane cleared his throat and grabbed Lucky's arm. "Though I think Lucky and I will just go out for breakfast."

"Oh, sorry. You don't need to do that." Robin blushed and shook her head. "Please don't leave because of me."

"No worries. It will give Lucky a break from cooking." Zane rubbed Lucky's back and she leaned into the crook of his arm. "You guys can come as well, if you want."

"That sounds great." Robin responded at the same time that I started shaking my head.

"Well, I guess we can go." I said reluctantly. I didn't want to leave the house. I just wanted to go back to bed and ravish Robin some more.

"You don't want to just keep me in the bedroom, do you, Noah?" Robin raised an eyebrow and Lucky laughed.

"You tell him," she giggled.

"Of course not." I kissed Robin again. "We have plenty of time to eat and then come back to the bedroom."

"Noah!" Both Robin and Lucky glared at me while Zane laughed.

"I didn't mean it like that." I put my hands up. "I was cornered into that statement."

"Really?" Robin looked up at me with a devious smile. "I didn't see anyone corner you."

"Well, you know." I laughed. "I'm a guy, it happens to us all the time."

"Sure." Robin laughed and backed away from me. "I'm going to go and shower. I'd love to go to breakfast. I have to get to work by noon."

"Oh, no." I groaned. "I wanted to spend the day with you."

"Sorry," she smiled sweetly. "I have to make money, and I took off yesterday after Zane came into the restaurant last week saying he really needed me to come and see you."

"I was wondering how Zane set that up yesterday." I laughed. "I'm glad to hear that it wasn't too complicated."

"I think I'm going to go shower as well." Lucky smiled. "Shall we go up, Robin?"

"Let's do it." Robin leaned up and gave me a long deep kiss before walking out of the kitchen. I watched her walk out and then turned to Zane who was giving me a bemused look.

"What's so funny?" I rolled my eyes at him.

"You look like you're sprung."

"Sprung? Who says that?" I laughed and sipped some of my coffee as my heart pounded.

"I say that." He laughed. "And trust me, I recognize sprung when I see it."

"Zane, every guy looks sprung after a night of good sex."

"You dirty dog." He winked at me. "I guess you have been in drought, huh?"

"I had sex in Palm Bonita." I laughed and shook my head. "Though this is not a conversation I want to have."

"Well, we both know we're Beaumonts." He laughed. "We can both get laid anywhere."

"It's not about the sex." I shook my head and rolled my eyes at him. "And if Lucky heard you right now she would kill you and then leave you."

"What's the point of leaving me if I'm dead?" He laughed, but then his eyes grew dark and more serious. "Seriously, though, I hope you know what you're doing. Sex is great, but Robin looks like she's not the sort of girl to just have casual sex."

"I'm not using her, Zane."

"I know you're not that type of guy, but you know, just be careful. I know things are complicated with you."

"Nothing's complicated." I lied.

"Does she know about the other girl?"

"What other girl?" I feigned ignorance.

"The one you dated in Palm Bonita?"

"We broke up, Zane."

"But there's still unresolved stuff there. I can tell."

"I don't want to talk about this right now." I shook my head. "I've got it handled."

"Sure you do." He sighed. "You may have the Beaumont sex appeal, but you also have the Beaumont knack of messing it up with girls."

"You got Lucky."

"Only because the gods were with me." He laughed. "I swear I must have done something right in my life."

"You're a good guy, bro." I said seriously. "She's lucky to have you as well."

"Sometimes I don't know if I'm good enough for her." All of a sudden he looked unsure of himself. "I love her so much, Noah. I never knew love could be like this. I still get overwhelmed sometimes. She's everything to me. She's my life. I'm so happy. You can thank her for me not killing you yesterday or today by the way. She's grounded me and made me feel whole in a way I never knew was possible."

"I don't know what to say." I stared at him. "I'm so happy for you. You've found a happiness that eludes many of us."

"You'll find it as well." Zane paused and was about to talk again when my phone started ringing.

"One moment." I reached for my phone and my heart stopped when I saw Skylar's number on the caller id. "Hello." I spoke into the phone softly. There was silence on the other side. "Hello. Skylar are you there?" I held my breath as I waited for her to reply.

"Hello," a voice whispered and I felt sweat break out in my face.

"Skylar?"

"Yes," she mumbled.

"Oh, my God, Skylar, are you okay?" I spoke into the phone quickly worried she was going to hang up on me again. I saw a movement from the corner of my eye and I realized that I was still in the kitchen with Zane. He was staring at me with a worried expression in his eyes and I turned around. I couldn't deal with him right now. I needed to concentrate on Skylar.

"Noah?"

"Yes, angel. It's me." I let out a deep breath. "Are you okay?"

There was silence on the other side of the phone and that I heard what sounded like sobs and I froze as my hand gripped the phone tightly.

"What's wrong?" My voice rose slightly. "Tell me what's wrong, Skylar."

"You left me." She sobbed, this time not hiding her tears.

"I didn't …"

"You didn't say goodbye," she sobbed into the phone. "I miss you, Noah."

"I didn't want to make it harder." I said slowly, not sure what to say. I had taken the coward's way out. Everything had gotten so bad and I had no recourse, and I knew that I just had to walk away.

"I love you." She cried harder. "You told me when people love each other, they are always there for each other."

"I am always here for you." I whispered into the phone. "I am always here for you, Skylar."

"My arm hurts." She stopped sobbing and her voice grew softer. "I have to go lie down because my arm hurts."

"What's wrong with it?"

"It got broke." She sighed. "It got broke when I bumped into the chair."

"Oh, my God," I closed my eyes. "You didn't bump into the chair, did you?"

"I bumped into the chair hard and it broke because I am clumsy." She said the words that she had been commanded to say.

"Skylar, tell me the truth, please. What happened to your arm?"

"You don't care," she whispered. "You left me."

"Skylar, please." My heart ached for her.

"I have to go and lie down now." She yawned. "I'm tired."

"Didn't you sleep last night? It's morning, Sky."

"I had to stay up last night and keep guard." She yawned again. "I'm sleepy and my arm hurts."

"Skylar, put Monica on the phone." I spoke quickly.

"No." she sounded scared.

"Please put Monica on the phone." I begged, praying she would do as I asked. But then I heard a click and realized that she had hung up. I stood there with the phone next to my ear for at least a minute before trying to call it back again. This time the phone went straight to voicemail and I knew she had turned it off. I stood there for a moment in a complete panic, not sure what to do, when Zane spoke.

"What's going on, Noah?" Zane looked at me with a concerned expression. "What was that call about?"

"Nothing." I shook my head, not knowing how to explain the situation to him. An idea was starting to form in my mind and the less he knew the better. If he didn't know anything, then the police couldn't accuse him of being an accessory to my plan.

"Noah, I'm not going to ask you again. What was that about?" Zane looked at me with a furious expression. "It sure didn't sound like nothing. It sounded like it was a lot more than nothing. Who is this Skylar and what does she have over you?"

"She doesn't have anything over me." I glared at him, my heart still pounding. All I could think about was how tinny her voice had sounded. And her arm. What had happened to her arm? I was pretty sure that whatever had happened hadn't been an accident. I needed to get her out of Palm Bonita even if it meant we had to be on the run.

"Noah." Zane grabbed a hold of my shoulders and looked into my eyes. "Are you in any trouble?"

"No. I'm not." I shook my head and attempted a smile. I needed to diffuse the situation or he was going to keep at it. And I didn't want to tell him anything. Part of my heart was splitting open as I realized that once again I would have to leave him without telling him what was going on. I couldn't risk him knowing the truth.

"Okay." He sighed. "Don't tell me now. But I sure hope you know what you're doing. You've got one girl upstairs in your shower and another one calling you on the phone and I've got a feeling that it's not a good idea to be playing both of them." He shook his head and walked out of the kitchen and I stood there frozen. I had almost forgotten about Robin. If I carried out my plan, that would mean the end for me and her and any possible relationship. I couldn't expect her to understand my tie to Skylar. I wasn't even going to try to explain it to her. I clenched my feelings as I realized that I was going to lose the chance to see what we could have been. I couldn't dwell on a relationship that hadn't even happened yet. I couldn't regret the future that wasn't to be. Not if I wanted to save Skylar. I pulled out my phone to call Sidney, to see if his son had found any loopholes in the law to allow me to carry out my plan without becoming a fugitive. The phone went to voicemail and I hung up without leaving a message.

"Noah, you still in here?" Lucky walked back into the kitchen, her long, wet hair hanging down her back. She gave me a concerned look. "Everything okay?"

"I take it Zane rushed right up to tell you about the call."

"No, of course not." She blushed and I knew she was lying.

"Lucky, I don't want to talk about it." I shook my head. "I'm going up to shower."

"Wait a second." She called out to me as I was leaving the room. "If you're in love with someone else, it's not fair to keep seeing Robin. It's not fair at all."

"I like Robin a lot. I'm not using her." I turned around and looked at her with bleak eyes. "We have a very special connection."

"As special as the connection you have with Skylar?"

"That's not fair. Like I told you before you have no idea what you're talking about."

"Then tell me, Noah. Tell me and Zane. Let us in. We may be able to help you sort it all out."

"Lucky, I would love to tell you both more than anything. But it's too risky." I shook my head. "I don't want either of you to get into trouble. I just …" I broke off as Lucky's face became even more worried. "I'm sorry, the less you know right now the better for you both."

"You're not going to do anything stupid, are you?"

"I always do something stupid." I sighed and gave her a half-smile. "Thanks for your concern, Lucky, but I'm going to take care of everything."

"Okay." She sighed and looked away. "Hey, can I borrow your phone quickly? I wanted to test the Facetime feature out with my phone. Just while you're in the bathroom?"

"I guess." I handed over my phone reluctantly. "If Sidney calls me, don't answer. I'll just call him back later."

"Okay, sure." She smiled and took the phone. "Oh wait, can you unlock it for me, please?"

"I guess so." I sighed as I punched in the numbers giving her access to my phone. For some reason I didn't think she was being honest about wanting to play around with Facetime, but I didn't really know what else she would want my phone for. "I'll see you in a few minutes."

"Take your time." She turned away from me and opened the fridge and I walked back to the stairs slowly. I felt like a fraud going back upstairs to Robin, pretending everything was the same as it had been just minutes ago. I felt nauseous walking up the stairs. Last night had been one of the best nights of my life. Making love to Robin had awakened something in me that I didn't know existed. I had felt truly alive for the first time in my life, but now I would never be able to explore that connection.

"Hey," Robin looked up at me as I opened the door. She was sitting on my bed, wrapped in a white towel and she was combing her hair. "I thought you went missing."

"Sorry, had a call and then had a chat with Zane."

"Is he okay?"

"Yeah," I walked over to the closet so that I could avoid looking at her. A part of me was already aching as I stared at her. "He's fine."

"I suppose that must have been a super big shock for him. I couldn't imagine finding out that my mother wasn't really my mother and that my real mother was dead."

"Yeah." I pulled out a shirt and jeans. "Life can be a bitch sometimes."

"That's true." Her voice was soft and I looked back at her. She was staring into space with a thoughtful look on her face.

"What about you? Where are your parents?"

"Not sure." She looked over at me with a wry smile. "My foster parents are in Ohio, but I have no idea where my real parents are."

"I didn't realize you were adopted."

"I wasn't adopted." She made a face. "Just fostered. Went through five different families until I hit thirteen and then stayed with the same family until I aged out of the system."

"That must have been hard." I walked over to her and sat on the bed next to her. "I'm sorry."

"It's not your fault." She shrugged. "The older I get the more I realize just how shitty some families can be. So maybe I got lucky. One of my foster fathers told me that my father used to beat my mother and then she killed him. I don't know if that is true, but I'm sure it's true for someone out there."

"I don't understand people sometimes." I clenched my fists. "Or men that hit women and children. Or women that hurt children."

"Abuse is horrible." Robin nodded and I looked at her quickly. "And no, I was lucky enough to have never been abused."

"Thank God."

"Yeah, I'm lucky that my last foster family was made up of two parents who really cared. They weren't just in it for the paycheck."

"Do you consider them your family?"

"Yeah." She paused and then looked at me with wet eyes. "They loved me. They supported me. They took care of me. It doesn't matter to me that they aren't my blood. I still love them with all my heart."

"Love isn't about what family you're born into." I pulled her into me. "Sometimes we form families with people we would never expect to."

"Have you ever—" She started to talk, but I leaned down and kissed her, not wanting to think about anything else. All that mattered right now was that we were together and we were bonding. All I wanted was to feel her lips under mine as I kissed her. I listened to her low moan and sigh and I couldn't stop myself from pulling her towel off and slipping my boxer briefs off at the same time.

"Oh, Noah," she moaned as my hand cupped her breast and squeezed. I pulled her down with me to the bed and allowed my body to enjoy the feel of her naked skin against mine. "We have to go to breakfast."

"I need you." I groaned as I continued to kiss and caress her. "I need to feel myself inside of you."

"You were inside of me all last night and this morning as well."

"Well, my body needs to feel you again. I'm thirsty and only you can quench my need."

"Oh, Noah," she giggled.

"Don't you want me as well?"

"Yes, I want you."

"What do you want?"

"I want to feel you inside of me, heating me up internally. I want to feel our two bodies become one," she whispered into my ear, and I pushed my erection up next to her, so that she could feel the urgency of my need.

"I want to fuck you, Robin. I want to make you mine," I groaned as she pushed her breasts up to my chest and pulled me down on top of her, spreading her legs and wrapping them around my waist.

"Take me, Noah. Take me." She moaned and then screamed as I entered her roughly. I thrust into her hard and fast. This wasn't a romantic fuck to show her how much I appreciated her body. This was a hard, rough, primal fuck to allow us both to connect and release our passions together. This was to let her know what my words couldn't tell her. This was for her to remember when I was no longer here. It was selfish of me, but I wanted my face to be the one she thought of when she was alone in her bed. I wanted her to remember the feel of me sliding in and out of her when she was ready to come. I needed to make sure she never forgot me.

***

"You guys took a while. I'm starving." Lucky gave me a look as we finally descended the stairs.

"Sorry, Robin was helping me scratch my back."

"Sure she was." Zane frowned at me and walked towards the front door. "Let's go eat."

"He okay?" Robin mouthed at me as we walked hand-in-hand to the door.

"He's always grumpy when he's hungry." I smiled at her and tried to ignore the feelings of guilt that had crept into my stomach.

"Will you spend the night at my place?" Robin looked up at me with an anticipatory look. "I know it may seems a bit fast, but I was hoping you could come over tonight, so you could see my place."

"I, uh, I'm not …" I stammered not knowing what to say.

"It's okay if you don't want to." She looked disappointed. "You can always come over some other time."

"It's not that I don't want to." We got into the car and she shifted away from me in the backseat. "I had something I was supposed to do tonight, but I can cancel and come over tonight."

"You don't have to do that." Her eyes lit up, but she still looked a bit uncertain. "I understand if you can't make it."

"No, no. I want to come." I scooted over to her, so that I could feel her warmth against me. "It will be fun. Plus, I will get to christen a new bed."

"That's why you want to come over?" She laughed, but I could see that she was happy that I was coming over. *What are you doing, Noah?* I screamed at myself inside. I had no idea why I was continuing to develop this relationship when I was likely going to be leaving Los Angeles forever in a couple of days. I didn't want to perpetuate a lie or have Robin hate me, but I didn't how to say no to her. Not when all I wanted to do was to see her smile and have her next to me.

"You guys okay with a pancake place?" Lucky looked back at me and her eyes were disapproving.

"Sounds good to me." I nodded and Robin licked her lips. "I think Robin's okay with it as well."

"Oh, remind me to give you back your phone when we get there." Lucky mentioned casually and I saw Zane giving her a quick look.

"Yeah." My stomach turned as I thought about the last phone call and everything that I was planning to do came crashing back down on me. "Did Sidney call at all?" I looked at Lucky and she shook her head. I looked out the window and panic suddenly filled me. All of a sudden I felt very alone and I wasn't sure who I could turn to or talk to. It hit me that I was making a mistake that could end up getting me imprisoned but then the other possibility was that something really bad could happen to Skylar. Maybe next time it wouldn't just be a broken or fractured arm. Maybe next time she would be even more seriously injured. I just couldn't take the risk. She meant too much to me. Skylar was a part of my heart, and when you loved someone, you never let them go.

"Hey, Noah. What you thinking about?" Robin squeezed my knee and I turned towards her slowly.

"You." I lied.

"Liar," she laughed and shook her head.

"You can read me already." I played with her hair.

"It's not hard. Your face is an open book." She snuggled into me. "It's one of the reasons I like you so much."

"You like me, huh?"

"Kinda, sorta." She grinned up at me. "I did invite you to my place, didn't I?"

"Kinda, sorta, huh? That's it?" I kissed her cheek and she shifted her face so that I was kissing her lips.

"Well, maybe a bit more than that." She grinned as she pulled away from me. "And maybe that bit isn't so little."

"Great." I grinned back at her and sat back feeling dazed. Part of me was excited that Robin was falling for me, really falling for me. But the other part of me wanted to scratch my eyes out for leading her on when I knew that nothing good could come out of our relationship. I closed my eyes to try and stop the guilt from spreading through my body.

"I can't wait until tonight," Sshe whispered in my ear, and I opened my eyes and turned to her.

"I can't wait as well." I held her hands as I stared into her eyes, trying to memorize her face. I was going to be selfish and spend one more night with her. And then I was going to leave. I had already decided that there was only one answer to the pain in my heart. I had to go to Palm Bonita and I had to take Skylar and we had to disappear. And I wouldn't be able to tell anyone my plan. Not if I wanted to keep Sklylar safe. If everything went as planned, we'd have to disappear off the face of the earth. I stared at Lucky and Zane chatting in the front seat and then at Robin as she sat next to me with a happy smile on her face. I should have been happy. I was finally surrounded by love and happiness. But I wasn't. I was sad. I was sad because I knew that this future, this life would forever elude me. I was not destined for the happily ever after like Zane was. I was destined to save a life. And if her safety meant giving up everything, it was something I had to do. I was Skylar's everything. I couldn't be the next in the long line of people to let her down and fail her forever. Walking away had already broken her heart. I couldn't allow her spirit to be broken forever as well.

"Hello," Lucky grabbed her phone as soon as it rang. "Yes, I called earlier and left a voicemail." Her voice was low as she spoke and I saw her look at me quickly before turning back to the front. "Can I call you back in about ten minutes please? A different number? Sure, hold on." She grabbed a pen and piece of paper from her bag. "Ready." She scribbled something down and then pushed paper back in her bag. "Got it, thanks. I'll call you back on the other number." She hung up the phone and pushed it into her bag."

"Who was that?" I asked her curiously.

"Oh, no one." She looked at me with a quick smile, as her face turned red. "Someone about a class I wanted to take at UCLA."

"I see." I didn't push the conversation, even though I was sure she was lying.

"I'm super hungry." Lucky changed the subject. "I could eat about ten pancakes." She laughed and Zane joined and laughed with her. I was about to say something else when Robin whispered in my ear. "I'd rather be eating big Noah."

I turned to her with a shocked expression and she grinned at me. "Maybe I'll get to eat him tonight."

CHAPTER TWELVE

"*Z* *ANE, WHY DID MOM LEAVE?"*
I whispered into the darkness of his room as I opened the door.

"I'm sleeping, Noah. Go to bed."

"Okay." I continued my walk into his room and sat down on his bed. "I was thinking she might be lost."

Zane remained silent and rolled over away from me, so I grabbed his shoulder and shook it excitedly. "I was thinking that maybe we should draw a map so she can find her way home again."

"Noah, if she can't find us, how are we going to give her a map?"

"We can post them in the grocery stores and on street lamps. We can put one on every corner."

"She's not going to see them and that's not going to work." Zane sat up and turned on his nightlight. "Just go to bed, Noah."

"I don't want to go to bed." I shook my head and snuggled in next to him. "And the maps will work. Those posters work to find missing kids, why can't it work to find Mom?"

"Mom isn't a missing kid," he sighed, exasperated.

"But she's lost and wants to come home." I whispered tightly. "We need to do everything that we can."

"I'm too tired to draw." He reached over and turned the light off. "You can sleep in my room tonight, but you have to be quiet."

"If I went missing, would you draw a map for me?" I whispered out aloud to the ceiling. "Would you look for me or would you go to sleep?"

There was more silence, and for a moment I thought Zane had fallen asleep. I felt sad and cold and I wanted to cry.

"Noah," Zane finally spoke and he turned around to face me. "If you went missing, I would search heaven and earth to find you. You're my brother. I will always be here to protect you and to love you. There is nowhere you could go and nothing you could do to stop me from loving you and being here for you. Absolutely nothing. If you went missing, my life would never be the same and I'd have to go missing as well, just so I could have a chance to find you."

"You can't go missing as well. What if I come back home?" I said matter-of-factly. "You have to be there to greet me."

"I'll always be here for you, Noah. I will always do everything in my power to make sure you are okay. If I sense anything is wrong, I will fix it."

"What if I don't tell you and I keep it to myself?" I said wide-eyed, deliriously happy that Zane was taking so much time to talk to me and show me how much he loved me.

"I will always know, Noah. Even if you keep it to yourself. I will always know when something is wrong. And I will always do whatever I can to make that situation right."

"You're like a magician" I yawned and snuggled under the duvet. "My very own magician brother."

"Sleep tight, Noah," he whispered. "I'll never let the bed bugs bite you."

"Did you have any foster brothers and sisters that you were close to?" I sat on Robin's cream couch as she poured two glasses of a bottle of Riesling for us. This was the second night I was spending at Robin's and I felt sad that it was likely the last night that either of us would have together.

"I had three sisters and three brothers." She handed me a glass and smiled. "However, they are all a lot older than me, so I'm not really close with any of them."

"It must have been hard growing up in foster care." I gave her a smile as she sat next to me. "Not really knowing where you came from and all that."

"It's hard." She nodded at me. "Some days, I just want to know what they looked like. What they did, why they gave me up. But then some days, I'm glad I don't know, because what if it was bad? I don't want to carry that burden with me."

"That makes sense," I agreed. "I was really worried about how Zane would feel about his birthmother's death. I was scared he would carry that burden and guilt forever."

"You guys are really close, aren't you?" She took a sip of wine and sat back. "It must be nice to have someone you're that close to."

"He's my best friend and my big brother. There's nothing I wouldn't do for him."

"Asides from tell him you're going to fake your own death." She teased me and I gave her a wry smile.

"Yeah, asides from that, I guess."

"Wasn't it hard keeping it a secret? I'm not judging you, but how could you do that?" She looked at me with wonder in her eyes. "Personally, if you had been my brother, I'm not sure I would have ever forgiven you. I hate being lied to, especially by the people closest to me."

"It was for my brother's safety." I started and she shook her head.

"That's bullshit." She took a sip of wine. "No offence, but you do realize that's bull. He's your brother and from what I know of him, he seems like a pretty great and trustworthy guy. You should have told him."

"Sometimes you have to lie to the ones you love to protect them." I gave her an earnest look as I said the statement Special Agent Waldron had instilled in me. "Sometimes the ones you love are better off not knowing the truth."

"What malarkey is that?" She shook her head vehemently. "You should never lie to the ones you love. What sort of foundation is that for a relationship built on love and honesty?"

"Sometimes you can't tell people everything." I shrugged and took a deep gulp of wine. I was starting to feel claustrophobic and I didn't know how much longer I could continue in this conversation.

"I don't agree." Robin looked upset and jumped up. "Do you want anything to eat? I have some turkey slices and some grapes."

"That sounds good, thanks." I nodded and sat back as she walked into the kitchen. I looked around the apartment and enjoyed the opportunity to have a glimpse into her soul. The apartment complex itself was sketchy, but her apartment was a real home. It smelled like peaches and pie and while everything was slightly worn, it wasn't tattered. It was lived in and homey. The only thing that I noticed was that there weren't a lot of photographs at all, and for some reason that surprised me. I looked at a console table with two frames and went over to look at the two photos. One appeared to be a photo of her and an older couple, whom I assumed to be her foster parents, but the next photograph was a photo of her with a man and he had her arm around her. I felt a surge of jealousy as I looked at the photograph. I wanted to know who the man was and why she still had his photo up in her apartment. Did she still love him? I wanted to go into the kitchen and demand that she tell me who he was, but I stopped myself from doing so. For one, I thought that only a crazy guy would go demanding answers when he wasn't even officially in a relationship, and secondly, I realized that this might be the last night I ever spent with her. Who was I to go act all jealous and then just leave? I already felt like scum staying the night at her apartment, knowing I was going to be leaving Los Angeles the next day. The phone call with Skylar was still at the forefront of my mind and I knew that I had to go and save her.

"Here we go," Robin walked back into the room with a smile. "I hope you're hungry, I put quite a bit on the plate."

"Thanks. I'm pretty starved." I sat back down on the couch and grabbed some grapes. "So who's the guy in the photo?" I pointed to the console and almost groaned to myself. I just couldn't stop the little green monster from coming out.

"Oh," Robin paused. "That's me and my ex. Sorry."

"No need to be sorry." I gave her a quick smile, trying to pretend I was not terribly disappointed. "Do you still love him and miss him, then?"

"No." She shook her head slowly. "Not really."

"So sometimes?" I leaned towards her.

"I guess." She sighed and sat back. "I don't have feelings for him anymore. But sometimes I miss him. We used to be friends."

"I see." I didn't see and I didn't want to do anything but smash the photo.

"Do you still miss your ex?" Robin looked at me curiously and her eyes were alert.

"No," I shook my head as anger raced through me. "I hate her." I sighed and then paused. "Well, no, I don't hate her. But I dislike the person she is. She's the sort of woman who makes you want to protect her because she acts like she's a victim, but really it's others who need protecting from her."

"Sounds like she really hurt you."

"She did hurt me." I said bitterly. "In her own way, she hurt me the best way she knew how."

"I'm sorry."

"Don't be. It's not your fault. She was married, you know. She escaped from her ex. She told me that he had been beating her. She even had some scars. She was really broken. I knew that from the start. I could see it in her face, hear it in her voice. We both were in Palm Bonita because we had to be, not because we wanted to be, and we both missed the outside world. That's how we bonded." I talked more than I had expected to, but I wanted Robin to understand. Maybe not today or tomorrow, but once she realized I was gone and why, I wanted her to remember this conversation and understand why I had to leave. I wanted her to know it wasn't because I didn't like her.

"That sounds pretty reasonable." She nodded, but I could see little sparks of jealousy in her eyes as well.

"We shared personal and intimate information about each other." I sighed. "I told her why I was really in Palm Bonita. I had wanted her to know I wasn't one of the bad guys. That I was really there for a good reason. I even told her who my father was and that I came from a family of money. I made all the mistakes I wasn't supposed to make. And she held it over me."

"She blackmailed you?" Robin gasped.

"No," I shook my head. "She was too smart for that. But she would ask for things or expect things. She would hold stuff over my head. She was smart, you know. She knew how to word things to make you wonder and feel sorry for her. And I fell for it."

"She doesn't seem like a very nice person."

"Oh, she wasn't." I sighed and shook my head. "She wasn't a nice person at all." I stared into Robin's eyes wanting to tell her everything so badly. But I was scared. I had made that mistake before and it had nearly cost me everything. I couldn't risk anything going wrong at this point. "Excuse me a second," I smiled at Robin as my phone rang and I answered it. "Hello, Lucky."

"Noah." Lucky's voice was low. "You need to come home."

"Why, what's wrong?" I said quickly and with worry. "Is it Zane?"

"No." She took a deep breath. "Zane and I did something."

"What did you guys do?" My heart pounded with fear and all I could think about was when Lucky had taken my phone a couple of days ago. "Did you call my mom?"

"No." She paused. "Zane, please you have to come home."

"Why, Lucky? Why?"

"Noah, Skylar's here."

I almost dropped the phone on the floor as shock fell over me. What was going on? "What do you mean Skylar's there? There's no way. How could she get there by herself?"

"She's not by herself."

"Oh, God." My face turned pale and my heart started beating fast. "Oh, my God."

"I'm sorry, Noah." She gulped. "I didn't know. We didn't know. We thought this would be good for you. I'm—"

"What did you do, Lucky?" I shouted in the phone, angrier than I had ever been in my life.

"Please just come home." She sobbed. "I don't want to be here alone with her."

"Where's Zane?"

"He's not at home."

"I'm on my way." I ended the call and turned to a worried-looking Robin. I pulled her up and towards me and looked her straight in the eyes. "I'm sorry, I have to go." I kissed her hard and tried to remember the taste of her lips and the smell of her hair as I held her close to me for a few moments.

"What's going on, Noah?" She looked at me with a scared expression. "What's wrong with Lucky?"

"I have to go." I said wildly grabbing my car keys. "My ex is here." I looked at her shocked and hurt expression but I didn't have time to explain everything to her. "I'm sorry but I have to go." I ran out of the door, without looking back and ran to my car quickly. I needed to get home before anything happened. I jumped into my car in both excitement and fear. I was excited that I would finally be reunited with Skylar but I was extremely worried about what else might go down. I took a deep breath and squared my shoulders. No matter what happened tonight, I wasn't going to let Skylar get hurt again. No matter what!

***

I walked into the house slowly. I was scared about what was going to happen. I didn't even really understand how they had both gotten there, but I had a feeling Zane and Lucky were to blame. I thought back to the last couple of days and the incident in the kitchen when I'd had the conversation with Skylar right in front of Zane, and how minutes later Lucky had conveniently wanted to borrow my phone. Then I remembered the call she had received in the car, and the new number she had taken down to call. It all clicked into my head. I was pretty sure I knew how they had gotten her. Zane and Lucky had most probably tried to help me out, but they had no idea what the situation was. They had no idea that they had most probably made the situation worse for me and Skylar. They had no idea who she was to me.

I had only been in the door for a few minutes when someone came running into my arms. "Noah, Noah, it's really you." She cried tears of joy as she jumped into my arms and I picked Skylar up and swung her around.

"It's really me, angel." I sat her down and kissed her on the cheek, staring at her beautiful and innocent face. She looked just the same as I remembered her, with her big wide blue eyes, the little button nose, and a big gap in her front teeth. I crouched down so that I was on eye-level with her and looked into her eyes. "I'm sorry that I left Palm Bonita without saying goodbye."

"You never came back to see me." Her eyes were wide and wet. "I thought I made you mad at me."

"You could never make me mad at you. I love you. You know that." I gave her a huge hug and my heart melted as she hugged me back tightly. As I hugged her, I wondered at the love I had for this child. This child who wasn't mine, but who had completely stolen my heart the very first time I'd met her.

"Well, now, now. Isn't this a cozy scene?" Monica walked up to us and gave us a haughty stare. "I always love to see my ex hugging my little bastard of a stepdaughter."

"Monica, not in front of Skylar." I covered the child's ears and glared at her. As I stared at her beautiful but evil face, I wondered how I had ever been taken in by her. She was most probably the worst person I had ever had the misfortune of dating. She had drawn me in with her smile and acting, but she had shown me her true colors pretty quickly after that. I'd wanted to break up with her a few months after we started dating, but I had already established a relationship with Skylar and I also knew that the only way I could look after Skylar and spend time with her was to keep on dating Monica.

"I don't know why you love that brat of a kid so much," she sneered at me, and then looked around the house with wide greedy eyes. "This place is so much more than I thought it would be. I guess you're as rich as you said."

"What do you want, Monica?" I glared at her before looking back down at Skylar. "Hey, honey, want to go play in the backyard?"

"Yes, please." She hugged my leg and then ran to the back. "Can I pick some flowers, Uncle Noah?"

"Of course." I beamed at her and waited until I saw her walk out the French doors to turn back to Monica. "What do you want?" I glared at her, and let my distaste show through.

"You better ask your new lover, Lucky. She's the one that called me."

"Lucky is my brother's fiancée." I shook my head in disgust.

"I'm sure you're fucking her." Monica leered at me as she stepped in closer to me. "Or maybe you've been missing me. Is that why I'm here? Been missing you."

"I've missed you as much as a good man misses hell."

"Noah, you're back." Lucky ran down the stairs and gave me a despairing and apologetic look.

"Yes." I nodded coldly.

"Where's Skylar?" She looked around wildly and I grabbed her arm.

"She's in the backyard." I nodded towards the back.

"She's a kid." Lucky looked at me with big eyes. "Skylar's a kid."

"Yes."

"So you really didn't miss your ex, did you?" Lucky chewed on her lower lip and I sighed.

"I told you that I didn't miss my ex." I sighed. "I told you you didn't really understand."

"I'm still here, bitches." Monica interrupted us. "Where the fuck is my money?"

"What money?" It took everything in me not to physically harm her.

"My money to go to Aruba," she sneered at me. "And no, I don't want you to come with me. You missed your opportunity."

"I have no interest in going with you anywhere."

"But for fucking Skylar, you'd go to the moon, right." She looked at me with thin eyes. "What a fucking weirdo you are. I should have known when you had to move to Palm Bonita you were a sicko."

"Skylar is like a daughter to me." My voice was low and angry. "I was the one who took her to the park, I was the one who took her bowling, I was the one who took her for ice cream. I was the one that made her feel safe again."

"You're also the one that left her crying for weeks on end." Monica looked at me with a gleam in her eye. "But I shut her up."

"You shut her up?" I frowned and then it hit me and I grabbed her arms and pushed her against the wall. "Did you break Skylar's arm?"

"She bumped into a chair." She looked at me with a blank stare. "And get your fucking hands off of me before I call the police."

"You're an evil bitch." I hissed at her before letting go of her arms.

"Noah!" Lucky walked up to me and grabbed me. "Calm down. Don't let her win." She whispered in my ear.

"I hate her so much." I said out loud. "You know how I tell you that all the dregs of society moved to Palm Bonita, well, she was the worst of them all. She is a thief, a con artist, an abuser. When I met Monica, I thought she was a victim of domestic violence. I thought she had fled an abusive husband. But I was wrong. Her husband was dead, had died in a car accident a few years before. Left her a couple hundred thousand. She spent that money then spent Skylar's college fund. Then she took jobs cleaning people's houses but she was also cleaning out their houses. She also conned several families out of their pensions with her schemes. Monica didn't flee to Palm Bonita because she was afraid of her ex-husband finding her and killing her, she fled because she was scared the cops would find her and imprison her for life."

"That's why you needed the private jet." Lucky's eyes popped open as she stared at Monica. "It wasn't because of your fear of flying with other people at all, was it?"

"Ding, ding ding. Your lover's a smart one," Monica cackled. "And I never lied to you, Noah. The very first day I met you, I told you there were lots of bad people in town and that you had to be careful. It's not my fault if you didn't listen to my advice."

"So what do you want, Monica?"

"I told your brother when he picked me up from the airport. He's very handsome, isn't he? So much more handsome than you. I'm sure he's better in bed as well."

Lucky glared at her, and I grabbed her hand so that she didn't try to slap Monica.

"What do you want?" I asked again, only this time my voice was a lot harder.

"What I've always wanted." She stared at me with a light expression. "Money."

"Why would we give you money?" I stared at her with hate.

"Because you love Skylar," she laughed, "and you don't want to see anything bad happen to her."

"You leave her alone," I moved forward to grab her again, but this time she reacted quickly and got out of the way.

"I'd be happy to leave her alone forever," she smiled at me, "for a million dollars."

"What?" My heart beat fast at her words. "What do you mean?"

"I'll sign over custody to you." She shrugged as if it were no big deal. "I couldn't give two shits about raising her. You love her so much then you can have her. Just give me a million dollars."

"I don't have a million dollars." My heart thudded as I stared at her. "My dad is the rich one. I don't have access to that kind of money."

"Oh, well, I guess it's back to Palm Bonita we go. Hopefully the next sucker to move to town can take care of me a little better than you did."

"Leave Skylar." I asked softly. "Leave Skylar with me. Even you have to know that's not the town for a little girl. And you're just not ready to be a mother."

"I'm ready to be a mother. I love kids," she screeched. "I want kids."

"Well, you're a mother now and you're not doing a great job." I shook my head.

"I'm not a mother." Monica gave me a look. "That little brat is not my kid. I married her dad after her mom died of breast cancer. She's not mine."

"She was your husband's child." My voice rose. "She is still your family. You should still love her. It doesn't matter if you don't have the same blood. You can still love someone with all your heart, even if you aren't biologically related."

"Oh, shut up, Noah. You always were an obnoxious prat. Save your holier than thou shit for church." She glared at me. "Where the fuck is my money?"

"I don't have a million dollars to give you, Monica," I sighed and shook my head. "Isn't there another arrangement we can come to?"

"I want a million dollars or Skylar leaves with me."

"I just told you. I don't have a million dollars."

"But I do." Zane's voice boomed as he walked into the room. I hadn't even heard the front door open,

I was so wrought with emotion. I stared at him as he walked up to me with a caring expression.

"Zane, you're back." I smiled at him weakly and he squeezed my shoulder. Lucky ran over to him and he put his arm around her holding her close.

"I have a cashier's check for you." Zane looked at Monica. "But get one thing straight, you're not getting this check until we go to an attorney and get the legal documents signed and taken care of."

"Let me see it." Her eyes bulged with happiness and greed.

"You'll see it only when we've been to the attorney." Zane's voice was firm.

"How do I know you're not lying?"

"I'm not in the habit of lying." Zane's tone was even. "But here, you can have a look." He opened his briefcase and took out a check and held it up for her. "I just got this from the bank and it's made out to you. You're lucky I have a good relationship with the bank manager and was able to get him to open the bank and do this for me. But here it is. One million dollars for you to do whatever it is you want to do. But you need to sign over full legal custody rights to Noah."

"I'll do it now if you want."

"We have to go to the attorney's office tomorrow." Zane shook his head. "Then you get the check."

"Fine. Where's my room?" she said sharply. "Or if you prefer, I can sleep with you."

"You'll sleep upstairs in a spare room." Zane looked at her in disgust. "And Lucky and Skylar will share a room tonight as well, so Lucky can make sure she's okay."

"Whatever." Monica shrugged and then looked at me. "I knew you were going to be a good catch."

"What does that mean?" I couldn't help but ask her the question.

"When I first saw you in Palm Bonita, I could tell you were a kind person. And then when you first met Skylar and were so sweet and gentle with her, I knew that you'd love her like a daughter. That is what I was hoping for. Why do you think I allowed you to take her out so much? I knew you'd help me kill two birds with one stone. I'm going to be a rich woman and I'm going to be rid of that brat."

"You're a horrible human being, you know that?" I looked at her in disgust and walked to the back garden so I could check on Skylar. "Hey, where are you?" I called out as I walked through the French doors.

"Right here, Uncle Noah," Skylar yawned up at me from the chair she was sitting on. "I was just taking a quick nap."

"I think it's time for bed, honey."

"I don't want to go to bed." She shook her head.

"But you're tired."

"I'm not tired." Her lower lip trembled.

"What's wrong?"

"I'm scared I'm going to wake up again and this will all be a dream." Tears slid out of her eyes. "I don't want to wake up and not see you."

"This isn't a dream, poppet. I'll be here in the morning. I'll be here every morning. I was coming to get you tomorrow. But instead, you came to get me first."

Skylar looked at me silently with big hopeful eyes and so I continued. "I made a mistake when I left you, Skylar. I didn't know how to say goodbye and I didn't know what Monica was going to say or do if I tried to take you with me. I tried to ask her to let me take you so I could give you a better life. But she threatened to do bad things. And because we're not family, I didn't have any legal rights, but I was trying, my love. I was always trying."

"I was so sad." She grabbed my hand. "I was so sad when you left."

"I'm so sorry, Skylar. But I promise I will never leave you again." I smiled at her and held her hand tightly. "I promise that I will always be here for you because when you love someone you will always be there for them; to protect them, to love them, to kiss them and hug them."

"Promise?"

"I promise." I heard my phone ringing and saw Robin's name on the screen before putting it back in my pocket. I didn't want to interrupt my time with Skylar by answering the phone. Not now. I hoped and prayed that

Robin would accept my call in a few days. But right now, all I could focus on was Skylar. She was finally going to become my daughter and this time, I had to make sure that I did everything in my power to keep her safe and make her feel loved.

***

"Here's to families." Zane's beer can clinked mine as we sat on the couch after dinner. It had been three days since we had met with the attorney and I was now in full legal custody of Skylar.

"Here's to me having the best family ever." I grinned back at him and took a chug of beer. "Thank you for being the best brother ever."

"It was the least I could do." He said and leaned back. "She's a great kid."

"She is." I agreed. "I sure hope I don't do anything to screw her up."

"You won't." Zane smiled at me. "And you know Lucky won't let you."

"That's true," I laughed. "She's already acting like a mom."

"I know." He groaned. "She's going to want ten kids now."

"You'll be happy to give them to her." I laughed and he chuckled.

"What about you? You want more?"

"I think that's a bit early to ask. I just became a dad and I don't even have a girlfriend." I laughed but I felt a little sad inside. Robin hadn't answered or returned any of the calls I had made in the last two days. I knew that I should have tried to explain everything earlier, but I had just been so overwhelmed.

"How's Robin?" Zane asked curiously and I shrugged. "Does she want to meet Skylar?

"She doesn't know about Skylar." I bit my lip and he looked at me in shock.

"Oh, boy." He shook his head. "You have to stop keeping things to yourself, bro. You're making it harder on yourself than you need to."

"I didn't want to get people involved with my worries." I sighed. "Especially not if I'm planning something that may be illegal."

"I knew you were up to no good." Zane shook his head. "As soon as I saw you on the phone, I knew you had some hair-brained plan up your sleeve."

"You didn't let on." I looked at him in surprise.

"I knew you wouldn't tell me what was going on." He sighed. "So I took matters into my own hands with the help of Lucky."

"I can't believe you guys did all that for me."

"I told you once before, Noah. I always sense when things are wrong with you. And I will always do everything in my power to make them right for you."

"Thank you, Zane." My voice was emotional. "I love you, bro. You know I used to think that only my future wife could show me how deep love could be. But your love and devotion for me, well, it almost breaks my heart. But in a good way. You make me believe that the bright side of love is the only side I should ever think and worry about. You make me believe that anything is possible." I took a deep breath and was about to continue when the doorbell rung.

"You should go and get that, bro." Zane jumped up and pulled me up.

"Who is it?"

"Open the door and go and see." He gave me a quick hug and walked away. "I'm going to go up and see if Lucky wants any help reading Skylar her bedtime story."

"Okay." I nodded at him and walked to the door slowly, my heart was pounding as I opened the door.

"Hi," she said with a tight smile.

"Hi," I replied, and opened the door wider to let her in. "It's good to see you, Robin."

"Zane said you wanted to talk? That it was an emergency?"

"Yes." I nodded, grateful that my brother had stepped in for me once again. "Yes, I'd love to talk. There are some things I want to tell you."

"Okay." She looked at me with hurt still in her eyes, and I knew that she was mad at me. I knew that she was upset that I hadn't confided in her earlier. I knew that I had cracked her veneer and it broke my heart.

"First off, I want to ask you a question." I took a deep breath. "Do you think that we could start again, from the beginning?" She looked at me, unspeaking, and I continued. "This time I want to get it right. This time I need to get it right. I know you're mad at me and you have every right to be, but I like you and I really want this to work. Please just tell me yes or no. Can we start again?"

Her eyes looked me over for a few minutes before she finally spoke. "Yes, Noah. We can start again."

AUTHOR'S NOTE

Thank you for reading *The Other Side of Love*. The last book in the *Forever Love* series is *Zane & Lucky's First Christmas*.

Please join my MAILING LIST to be notified as soon as new books are released and to receive teasers (http://jscooperauthor.com/mail-list/). I also love to interact with readers on my Facebook page, so please join me here: https://www.facebook.com/J.S.Cooperauthor. You can find links and information about all my books here: http://jscooperauthor.com/books/!

As always, I love to here from new and old fans, please feel free to email me at any time at jscooperauthor@gmail.com.

List of J. S. Cooper Books

Scarred

Healed

The Last Boyfriend

The Last Husband

Before Lucky

The Other Side of Love

Zane & Lucky's First Christmas

Crazy Beautiful Love

The Ex Games 1, 2 and 3

The Private Club 1, 2 and 3

ABOUT THE AUTHOR

J. S. Cooper was born in London, England and moved to Florida her last year of high school. After completing law school at the University of Iowa (from the sunshine to cold) she moved to Los Angeles to work for a Literacy non profit as an Americorp Vista. She then moved to New York to study the History of Education at Columbia University and took a job at a workers rights non profit upon graduation.

She enjoys long walks on the beach (or short), hot musicians, dogs, reading (duh) and lots of drama filled TV Shows.

Printed in Great Britain
by Amazon.co.uk, Ltd.,
Marston Gate.